William Montgomery Clemens

Famous Funny Fellows

Brief biographical sketches of American humorists

William Montgomery Clemens

Famous Funny Fellows
Brief biographical sketches of American humorists

ISBN/EAN: 9783337011901

Printed in Europe, USA, Canada, Australia, Japan

Cover: Foto ©Raphael Reischuk / pixelio.de

More available books at **www.hansebooks.com**

FAMOUS

FUNNY FELLOWS

BRIEF BIOGRAPHICAL
SKETCHES OF AMERICAN HUMORISTS

BY

WILL M. CLEMENS

CLEVELAND, OHIO
WILLIAM W. WILLIAMS
1882

CONTENTS.

4 CONTENTS.

FAMOUS FUNNY FELLOWS.

INTRODUCTION.

The rollicking newspaper humor of the day is of modern origin. It is even yet young in years. Humorists and newspaper wits were once—say a score of years ago—considered a rarity in America. At that time humor of the day meant the productions of a very few—Mark Twain, Joe Neal, Artemus Ward, Major Jones, and one or two others. To-day it means a certain *jeu d' esprit* that can readily be discovered in almost every first-class newspaper extant. In fact, every American journal of any prominence possesses its salaried paragrapher, who is required to produce, at stipulated intervals, a certain quantity of original humor, whether or no the said paragrapher be in a humorous mood.

A paragrapher is a writer of paragraphs, and paragraphs, in an American newspaper, are commonly understood to be short, concise, spicy and readable gems of wit and humor. In undertaking to present, in printed form, brief biographical sketches relative to the life, character, and works of representative American humorists, I entered into the work with the idea of entertaining and pleasing the American public at large, and not with the intent of delighting the individual humorist.

The volume that I offer to the reading public is the work of two years, or at least a portion of that time. When I first began on the work I wrote to Mark Twain, asking for a brief introduction, thinking that such an acquisition to the book, coming from such a source, would be highly valuable. At the time of receiving my letter the genial humorist was busily engaged putting the finishing touches to his Tramp Abroad, and he, as a result, cruelly—I will not say wantonly—cut me off with a shilling. However, I give Twain's reply to my communication, for, notwithstanding its briefness, the epistle contains at least one small grain of that peculiar wit for which the funny man of Hartford is noted. Here it is:

"HARTFORD, CONN., Nov. 18, 1879.
"WILL M. CLEMENS:

"My Dear Friend—Your letter received. Lord bless your heart! I would like ever so much to comply with your request, but I am thrashing away at my new book, and am afraid that I should not find time to write my own epitaph in case I was suddenly called for.

'Wishing you and your book well, believe me,
Yours truly,
SAMUEL L. CLEMENS."

There being such a vast field from which to select the titles to these sketches, I have, perhaps, unintentionally omitted or neglected a certain few of the great and growing circle of funny men. I have also omitted, intentionally, such humorists as Irving, Bret Harte, and others of a like stamp, who do not, in any sense, belong to the class of newspaper humorists.

W. M. C.

CLEVELAND, OHIO, 1882

SAMUEL LANGHORNE CLEMENS.

Routledge, in his Men of the Time, says that
Samuel Langhorne Clemens, better known by the
nom de plume of Mark Twain, was born in Florida,
Monroe county, Missouri, November 30, 1835.
During the last ten years newspaper reports have
made Mark Twain the native of a dozen different
localities.   According to these reports Mark has
been born in Adair county, Kentucky; in Fentress
county, Tennessee; in Hannibal, Missouri; and in
various other places.   However, it is proper for
me to state that Mark was born in but one·place,
and all at one time.   Routledge is evidently correct
as to both time and place.

The parents of Mark Twain were married in
Kentucky and lived for some years in that State.
His mother states that he was always an incor-
rigible boy, filled with roving imaginations from
his very earliest age, and could never be persuaded or forced to attend to his books and study,
as other boys did.   He lost his father at the age
of twelve, and soon after left school for good.

When about fifteen years of age, Mark came into
the house one day and asked his mother for five
dollars. On being questioned as to what he
wanted with it, he said he wanted it to start out
traveling with. He failed to obtain the five dollars, but he assured his mother that he would go
all the same, and he really went, nor did the old
lady ever set eyes on him again until he had become a man. Starting out on his travels he
learned the printing business, and supported himself by working at the case.

Clemens was but seventeen when he resolved
to become a steamboat pilot on the Mississippi
river. He learned the river in due time from St.
Louis to New Orleans, a distance of 1,375 miles,
and followed the occupation of pilot until he was
twenty-four years old. In 1861 an elder brother
was appointed Lieutenant-governor of Nevada
Territory. He offered Mark the position of private secretary, and the young man deserted the
river and went West. After a few months he
abandoned the life of a private secretary, and
started out to seek a fortune in the mines. In
this he was unsuccessful, although at one time, for
the space of a few minutes, Mark owned the
famous Comstock lode, and was worth millions.
He found all this out after he sold the claim.

After this, Clemens became a reporter and cor-

respondent, writing to the Territorial Enterprise
and other papers, and occasionally doing work at
the case. He wrote at times over the *nom de*
plume of Mark Twain, a title he adopted from his
experiences as a pilot It was during these years,
between 1862 and 1866, that Mark perpetrated
many broad and practical jokes, using his journalistic position as a channel. These publications.
gave him considerable notoriety in the West, and
especially on the Pacific coast. For several years.
he was local editor of the Virginia City Enterprise, but in 1864 he removed to San Francisco,
where he was offered a good position on a paper
there. In 1865 he went to the Sandwich Islands,
to write up the sugar plantations. His letters.
were very readable and were published mostly in
the Sacramento Union. All this time Mark was
struggling with legitimate literary work, and published occasional sketches in literary weeklies,
which were widely copied On his return from,
Hawaii he lectured for a short time in California
and Nevada. Some of his sketches having attracted attention in the East, Mark sailed for New
York in the early part of 1867, and published a
small volume of sketches, entitled The Celebrated
Jumping Frog of Calaveras, and Other Sketches.
The book sold well in the United States, and was
afterwards republished in England. Nearly all.

the sketches that appeared in the book had previously been published in the San Francisco papers.

In 1868, Mr. Clemens formed one of a party who sailed in the steamship Quaker City, for an extended excursion to Palestine and the Holy Land. He went in the capacity of a newspaper correspondent as well as for pleasure, and wrote interesting letters while abroad to the California papers. Returning to America he gathered his letters together and re-wrote them in book form, which he called Innocents Abroad, or the New Pilgrim's Progress. The work was very funny, yet notwithstanding the rollicking satire, and laugh-provoking character of the book, the author met with the greatest difficulty in getting it published. He sent his manuscript to the leading publishers of New York, Boston, and Philadelphia, and they all refused it. Mark's literary vanity was sorely wounded, and he was about determined to throw his book into the fire when a literary friend, Albert D. Richardson, now deceased, to whom he handed the manuscript, pronounced it very clever and offered to take it with him to Hartford, Connecticut, where was located the American Publishing Company, a firm that had issued several books for Richardson. After much talk and discussion among the directors of the

publishing company; the book was finally issued.
Its success was extraordinary, and since its publication over 200,000 copies of the book have been
sold. The publishing company cleared $75,000
by the venture.

In 1869 Twain tried journalism for a time in
Buffalo, where he held an editorial position on a
daily paper. While there he fell in love with a
young lady, a sister of "Dan"—made famous in
Innocents Abroad—but her father, a gentleman
of wealth and position, looked unfavorably upon
his daughter's alliance with a Bohemian literary
character.

"I like you," he said to Mark, "but what do I
know of your antecedents? Who is there to answer for you, anyhow?"

After reflecting a few moments, Mark thought
some of his old California friends would speak a
good word for him. The prospective father-in-law
wrote letters of inquiry to several residents of San
Francisco, to whom Clemens referred him, and
with one exception, the letters denounced him
bitterly, especially deriding his capacity for becoming a good husband. Mark sat besides his fiancee
when the letters were read aloud by the old gentleman. There was a dreadful silence for a moment,
and then Mark stammered: "Well, that's pretty
rough on a fellow, anyhow?"

His betrothed came to the rescue however, and overturned the mass of testimony against him by saying, "I'll risk you, anyhow."

The terrible father-in-law lived in Elmira, New York, and there Mark was married.   He had told his friends in the newspaper office at Buffalo, to select him a suite of rooms in a first-class boarding house in the city, and to have a carriage at the depot to meet the bride and groom.   Mark knew they would do it, and gave himself no more anxiety about it.   When he reached Buffalo, he found a handsome carriage, a beautiful span of horses and a driver in livery.   They drove him up to a handsome house on an aristocratic street, and as the door was opened, there were the parents of the bride to welcome them home.   The old folks had arrived on the quiet by a special train. After Mark had gone through the house and examined its elegant finishings, he was notified officially that he had been driven by his own coachman, in his own carriage, to his own house. They say tears came to his wonderfully dark and piercing eyes, and that all he could say was "Well, this is a first-class swindle."

Not long after his marriage, Mark settled down in Hartford, and invested capital in insurance com- panies there.   His second book, Roughing It, appeared in 1871, and had almost as large a sale as its predecessor. He visited England a few months later, and arranged for the publication of his works there in four volumes. On his return he issued his third book, in partnership with Charles Dudley Warner, which was styled The Gilded Age. This was followed by the Adventures of Tom Sawyer, a book for boys, in 1876. These books all commanded an immense sale, and several editions have been exhausted. The American Publishing Company of Hartford represented these works in this country, Chatto & Windus published them in England, and Mark's continental publisher was Tauchnitz of Leipzig.

April 11, 1878, Mark Twain sailed for Europe on the steamship Holsatia. He was accompanied by his family, and after drifting about for some months on foreign shores, settled down to spend the summer in Germany. In 1879 he returned to his home in Hartford, and after several months of work produced another book, A Tramp Abroad. This work had a ready and a very large sale, and has become quite popular. In 1881 he issued another book through a Boston house, The Prince and Pauper. This also has had a large sale in this and other countries.

Among his other accomplishments Clemens is a politician, and has done good service on the stump for the Republican party. For all this he is the proud possessor of the title of Honorable.

Many of the most ludicrous scenes in the works of Mark Twain are taken from life. The steam-boat scene in the adventures of Colonel Sellers, was witnessed by him when a young man. His adventure with a dead man was in his father's office in Missouri. His description of the horror creeping over him, as he saw a ghastly hand lying in the moonlight; how he tried to shut his eyes and tried to count, and opened them in time to see the dead man lying on the floor stiff and stark, with a ghastly wound in his side, and lastly how he beat a terrified retreat through the window, carrying the sash with him, is vividly remembered by every reader of The Gilded Age. The whole thing transpired just as Mark recorded it—the man was killed in a street fight almost in front of Mr. Clemens' door, was taken in there while a *post mortem* examination was held, and there left until the next morning. During the night Mark came in, and the scene he described was really enacted.

The Clemens mansion in Hartford is a model of architectural beauty, and is elegantly finished in the interior. In the library, over the large fire-place, is a brass plate with the inscription in old English text: ''The ornament of a house is the friends who frequent it.'' Mark does not use the library for his study, but does nearly all his writing in the

billiard room at the top of the house.   It is a long
room, with sloping sides, is light and airy, and
very quiet.   In this room Mark writes at a plain
table, with his reference books lying scattered
about him.   He makes it an invariable rule to do
a certain amount of literary work every day, and
his working hours are made continuous by his not
taking a mid-day meal.   He destroys much manuscript, and it is said he rewrote five hundred pages
of one of his popular books.   Mark is an industri-
ous worker, and continues his labors the year
round.   In summer he retreats to his villa on the
Hudson, or to a little cottage in the mountains
near Elmira, New York.   There he finds the
most quiet solitude, and there he works un-
disturbed.   Mark is fond of his home life, and
of his three beautiful children.   He has achieved a
notable success as a lecturer, both in this country
and in England.

The humor of Mark Twain is never forced.   It
bubbles up of its own accord, and is always fresh.
In his recent books he shows less of genuine wit
than in his earlier works perhaps, but yet his
writings are always readable.   He sent me, not long
since, a printed slip of his biography, taken from
Men of the Time, and on the margins of this
appeared the following *bon mot:*

"My Dear Clemens:

"I haven't any humorous biography—the facts don't admit of it. I had this sketch from Men of the Time printed on slips to enable me to study my history at my leisure.   S. L. Clemens."

There is a popular feeling abroad in the land to the effect that Mark Twain is a very funny man, and that he is seldom sober.   This is a grave mistake.   Mr. Clemens is by nature a very serious, thoughtful man.   True he seldom writes that which is not humorous, but occasionally he pens a very careful, serious communication, like the following for instance, which he addressed to a young friend of mine :

"Hartford, January 16, 1881.

"My Dear Boy:—How can I advise another man wisely, out of such a capital as a life filled with mistakes? Advise him how to avoid the like? No—for opportunities to make the same mistakes do not happen to any two men. Your own experiences may possibly teach you, but another man's can't. I do not know anything for a person to do but just peg along, doing the things that offer, and regretting them the next day. It is my way, and everybody's.

"Truly yours,
                 S. L. Clemens."

A writer in the San Francisco Chronicle wrote, not many years since, as follows: ''There have been moments in the lives of various kind hearted and respectable citizens of California and Nevada, when, if Mark Twain were up before them as members of a vigilance committee for any mild crime, such as mule stealing or arson, it is to be feared his shrift would have been short. What a dramatic picture the idea conjures up, to be sure! Mark, before those honest men, infuriated by his practical jokes, trying to show them what an innocent creature he was when it came to mules, or how the only policy of fire insurance he held had lapsed, and how void of guile he was in any direction, and all with that inimitable drawl, that perplexed countenance, and the peculiar scraping back of the left foot, like a boy speaking his first piece at school. It is but fair to say that the fun Mark mixed up for citizens in those days, was not altogether appreciated in the midst of it, for some one, touched too sharply, *surge bat amari aliquid*, and Mark had another denouncer joined to the wounded throng. . . . . . He is keenly sensitive to sympathy or criticism, and relates, as one of the most harrowing experiences of his life, a six hours' ride across England, his fellow traveler an Englishman, who, shortly after they started, drew forth the first volume of the English edition of Innocents Abroad from his pocket, and calmly perused it from beginning to end without a smile. Then he drew forth the second volume and read it as solemnly as the first. Mark says he thought he should die, yet John Bull was probably enjoying it after his own undemonstrative style."

In another instance the same writer says of Mark Twain: "This literary wag has performed some services which entitle him to the gratitude of his generation. He has run the traditional Sunday-school book boy through his literary mangle and turned him out washed and ironed into a proper state of flatness and collapse. That whining, canting, early-dying anæmic creature was the nauseating model held up to the full-blooded mischievous lads of by-gone years as worthy their imitation. He poured his religious hypocrisy over every honest pleasure a boy had. He whined his lachrymose warnings on every playground. He vexed their lives. So, when Mark grew old enough he went gunning for him, and lo, wherever his soul may be, the skin of the strumous young pietist is now neatly tacked up to view on the Sunday-school door of to-day as a warning, and the lads of to-day see no particular charm in a priggish, hydropathical existence."

Samuel Langhorne Clemens is in the high tide

of his success.   He is yet a young man, as far as the literary life goes.   Outside of his book making, he has given the fun-loving public some admirable things in the way of wit and humor through the pages of the leading magazines.   The originality of his writings in the past is retained in his work of the present, and he gives promise of many original things in the future.   He has a liking for the monotonous labor of literary work, his health is as yet unimpaired, he has been fortunate in love and in financial affairs, is consequently happy, and will yet give to the world of letters many quaint, bright, and original ideas.   Artemus Ward and Mark Twain are without a doubt the two leading humorists of the present century.   While we have the Artemus that was, we possess the Mark that is.   He leads the van of humorists who eke out an existence in the present.   He is the prince of funny men.   Long live the prince.

CHARLES FARRAR BROWNE.

Probably no writer in America—or out of it, for that matter—ever attained such universal notoriety, in such a brief space of time, as did that king of American humorists, Artemus Ward. His career was short but successful, and his fame will live as long as does the English language. Charles Farrar Browne was born in the hamlet of Waterford, Maine, on the 26th day of April, 1834, and died at Southampton, England, March 6, 1867. After graduating from the free village school at Waterford he sought and obtained employment in a printing office. As a printer's apprentice he traveled throughout the New England States, stopping for a brief period at one place and then another. Finally Charles settled down in Boston, where he obtained employment as compositor in the office of a weekly paper. He soon after began to compose comic stories and essays for different periodicals, which met with medium success.

Browne remained there but a short time, however, being of a roving disposition, and a few months later he gave up his idea of settling in Boston and left for the West, with but one suit of clothes (those were on his back) and with a few cents in his pocket. He obtained work as local reporter on papers in Cincinnati and Toledo, Ohio, and finally brought up at Cleveland in 1857, in which city he obtained a situation as reporter on the morning Plain Dealer. His old associates in Cleveland tell me that Browne at this time was considered one of the characters of the town. His dress was always shabby and scant ; his habits irregular, and his general appearance that of a country "greenhorn." He delighted in wearing on his head a large crowned slouch hat, and his pantaloons were as a rule nearly a foot too short for him. Being tall, slim, and bony, his appearance in those days as he slouched along the streets of Cleveland in search of items could not have been very prepossessing, to say the least. "He was then," says a well known humorist, "a mild-mannered, sunny-tempered young fellow of twenty-three, who delighted in witty anecdotes, and told droll stories in an inimitable way."

Despite his looks, Browne was a brilliant and ready writer. He became involved in numerous journalistic quarrels, and his cutting remarks and timely rebukes to his cotemporaries soon made known the fact that he could not be mastered.

A. Miner Griswold, the Cincinnati humorist,
tells the following story of Browne at that time :
"The first night of our acquaintance he took me
to a school exhibition on Cleveland heights, and
his whispered comments upon the performance
amused me greatly. They gave a portion of the
play of Rolla: 'How now, Gomez, what bringest
thou ?' Gomez: 'On yonder mountain we sur-
prisèd an old Peruvian.' Said Brown in a whisper,
'They knew him by his bark, a small bundle of
which you perceive he carries on his shoulder.'
There have been many Peruvian bark jokes since,
but that was then fresh to me—too fresh, perhaps.
But one finds plenty of funny people at twenty-
two, and I little dreamed that my entertainer, the
green young man by the name of Browne, was
destined to make the whole world laugh, and
weep, too, when it heard of his death. It did
occur to me as we drove back in the buggy that
my new friend was the least bit eccentric. After
riding along in silence for a time he suddenly
declared that he liked me, and asked me if I had
any objections to one embrace. Then he at-
tempted to throw his arms around me, but owing
to the darkness, I suppose, he embraced a new
plug hat that I wore, and when he let go it was
crushed into a shapeless mass. He apologized
profusely when he discovered what he had done,

appeared to give way to a momentary burst of tears, and then said that Shakespeare wouldn't have succeeded as a local editor, because he hadn't the necessary fancy and imagination.

"Barring an unreasonable desire to drive off the canal bridge into the water, which I prevailed upon him to relinquish with some difficulty, we reached the city without further incident. His humorous account of the school exhibition in the next day's paper confirmed me in the impression that the young man by the name of Browne possessed a rare streak of original humor."

The following autumn Browne published his first "Artemus Ward" letter that was extensively copied, an account of the Atlantic cable celebration in Baldwinsville; followed soon after by the Free Lovers of Berlin Heights, and later his letters from "Artemus Ward, showman," appeared, which attracted general attention.

In the early part of 1860, Browne surrendered his position as city editor of the Plain Dealer, and left Cleveland for New York. In the metropolis he was engaged as a contributor to Vanity Fair, a comic weekly paper that had but recently been established. Vanity Fair was a success for a time, but it was not lasting. Some months after his arrival in New York, Browne was offered the position as editor of the publication, and after some hesitancy, he accepted. The paper suspended soon after, and the young humorist was thrown upon his own resources once again. Several positions were offered him on various New York journals, but he concluded to give up journalism for a time and turn his attention to lecturing.

His first lecture, which was of a humorous nature, was delivered in New York city, December 23, 1861, and was well received. As a lecturer he was at once acknowledged as a success, and immediately delivered his mirth provoking orations in various parts of the country. In 1862 he published his first book, entitled Artemus Ward, His Book. In 1863 he paid a visit to the Pacific coast, making an overland trip, visiting Salt Lake city, and addressing large audiences wherever he stopped.

Returning to New York city in 1864, he opened his illustrated lectures on California and Utah with immense success. About this time his other books, Artemus Ward Among the Mormons, and Ward Among the Fenians, appeared. In 1866 he was prevailed upon by his friends to visit England, where he became a regular contributor to Punch, and gave his lecture on the Mormons, in the British metropolis. But while he was convulsing all London with laughter he was fast falling a victim to consumption, and becoming worse he went to Guernsey in 1867 for the benefit of his health. He became no better, and when he was just about preparing to return to America, he died at Southampton, March 6, 1867. By his will, after providing for his mother, leaving legacies to his friends, and his library of valuable books to a school-boy friend in his native village, he left the bulk of his property in trust to Horace Greeley for the purpose of founding an asylum for printers.

Mark Twain, in a private letter to a friend in Tennessee, says of Artemus Ward :

"He was one of the kindest and gentlest of men, and the hold he took on the English people surpasses imagination. Artemus Ward once said to me gravely, almost sadly :

"'Clemens, I have done too much fooling, too much trifling ; I am going to write something that will live."

"'Well, what for instance?

"In the same grave way, he said :

"'A lie.'

"It was an admirable surprise. I was just ready to cry; he was becoming pathetic."

There have been hundreds of stories of Artemus Ward going the rounds of the American press during the past twenty years. A few of them are founded on facts, some of them are good, but many, I am sorry to say, are base fabrications. This is not the case, however, with the little reminder that certain residents of Pottstown, Pennsylvania, are wont to tell. Ward was advertised to deliver his famous lecture on the Mormons, in the town hall, at Pottstown, during the winter of one of the earlier years of the war. Much curiosity was excited by the announcement of his coming, and there was every reason to expect that the hall would be crowded on the evening of the lecture. A fierce snow storm raged all day, however, and the night was wild and stormy. When the lecturer was driven to the hall, he found waiting for him only five men, who had defied the storm. Advancing to the stage, and beckoning with the finger, as to a single individual, Artemus said, in an ordinary conversational tone:

"Come up closer."

Not knowing precisely what to do, the audience of five compromised with their embarrassment by doing nothing. Artemus changed his tone to that used by one who wished to coax, and said:

"Please come up closer, and be sociable. I want to speak to you about a little matter I have thought of."

The audience, thus being persuaded, came up a little closer, and the humorist said:

'" I move that we don't have any lecture here this evening, and I propose instead that we adjourn to the restaurant beneath and have a good time."

Ward then put the motion, voted on it himself, declared it carried, and, to give no opportunity for an appeal from the chair, at once led the way to the restaurant. There he introduced himself to his intended auditors, and spent several hours in their company, richly compensating them for disappointment in the matter of the lecture, by the wit and humor of the stories that he told. That was how Artemus Ward lectured in Pottstown.

Glancing hurriedly through Ward's volume of sketches, I find none more amusing than his description of

THE CENSUS.

The sences taker in our town being taken sick, he deppertised me to go out for him one day, and as he was too ill to give me information how to perceed, I was consekently compelled to go it blind. Sittin' down by the roadside I draw'd up the follerin' list of questions, which I proposed to ax the people I visited:

Wat's your age?

Whar' was you born?

Air you married, and if so, how do you like it?

How many children hav' you, and do they suffi-

ciently resemble you so as to proclood the possi-
bility of their belongin' to any of your nabers ?

Did you ever have the measles, and if so, how
many ?

Hav' you a twin brother several years older than
yourself?

How many parents have you?

Do you read Watt's Hymns reg'lar?

Do you use bought'n tabacker ?

Wat's your fitin' weight ?

Air you troubled with biles ?

How does your meresham culler ?

State whether you air blind, deaf, idiotic, or got
the heaves ?

Do you know any Opry singers, and if so how
much do they owe you ?

What's the average of virtoo in the Ery canawl ?

If four barrels of emtin's pored onto a barn
floor will kiver it, how many plase can Dion
Boucicault write in a year ?

Is beans a reg'lar article of diet in your family?

How many chickens hav' you, on foot and in
the shell ?

Air you aware that Injiany whisky is used in
New York shootin' galrys insted of pistols, and
that it shoots furthest ?

Was you ever at Niagry Falls ?

Was you ever in the penitentiary ?

State how much pork, impendin' crysis, Dutch
cheese, poplar survinity, standard poetry, children's strainers, slave code, catnip, red flannel,
ancient history, pickled tomatoes, old junk, per-
foomery, coal ile, liberty, hoopskirts, etc., have
you got on hand?

But it didn't work. I got into a row at the
first house I stopt at, with some old maids. Dis-
believin' the answers they give in regard to their
ages I endeavored to open their mouths and look
at their teeth, same as they do with horses, but
they floo into a violent rage and tackled me with
brooms and sich. Takin' the sences requires experience, like as any other bizness.

Browne had few if any enemies, and hosts of
friends. Everyone with whom he became acquainted became his friend. He was as genial as
he was humorous, and his former companions
who are yet alive look back upon the time when
Artemus Ward, the king of American humorists,
took their proffered hand and shook it warmly in
his original and friendly way.

CHARLES HEBER CLARK.

On the eastern shore of Maryland is situated a
town known to the post-office authorities as Berlin.   It was in Berlin in the warm month of July,
1841, that Charles Heber Clark, "Max Adeler,"
first saw the light of day.

His father was a clergyman in the Episcopal
church, but this appeared to have little effect
on Charles, who, like all bad boys, grew up to
make fun of everybody and everything.   He was
sent to Georgetown, District of Columbia, early
in life, being shipped by express and labeled
"handle with care."   He attended school for a
brief period, learning but little, and jumped into
the mercantile world by moving his linen to Philadelphia.

The mercantile business appeared to agree with
his constitution until 1865, when he bethought
himself that he had been sent into this wicked
world for the express purpose of becoming a
journalist.   He subsequently began his editorial
career on the Philadelphia Enquirer during that

same year. Clark made rapid advancement in journalism, and in 1867 became one of the editors of the Evening Bulletin, of which paper he is at present one of the proprietors.

It was soon after Clark entered upon his editorial duties at the Bulletin office that the droll humor of his pen began to attract general attention. His most amusing articles were written in the intervals of his private life, and the more serious daily newspaper work to which he devoted himself. He is not, and never was, a paragrapher, but has thrown out to the world his droll and grotesque humor in the form of narratives. His fun is of the most rollicking kind, and ranks him along with Mark Twain and Artemus Ward. Three volumes of· humor have appeared from his pen.

His best known books are Out of the Hurly Burly, and Elbow Room. These works appeared several years ago simultaneously in this country and in England. The sales were large, and over five thousand copies of Elbow Room were sold in London within a month after its publication. Both books have been issued in Canada, where the piratical publishers sold them by the thousand.

His latest work, issued quite early in 1882, entitled The Fortunate Island and Other Stories, is meeting with a wide sale. It is destined to become very popular. Mr. Clark is fond of his home and family. His residence is located in a remote but beautiful suburb of Philadelphia, where he hopes to live to a ripe old age. Mr. Clark is an excellent musician, and for a number of years he acted in the capacity of organist for one of the Quaker City churches.

Besides his book-making Mr. Clark still retains a firm hold on journalism. He takes a leading interest in his paper, the Bulletin, and writes the dramatic criticisms and a portion of the editorials. He also edits the humorous department of Our Continent, a well-known literary weekly, published in Philadelphia.

As a writer and composer of obituary verse Max Adeler has probably no equal, unless it be another, older, and more prominent Philadelphia journalist—Childs, of the Ledger. The following rare exotics are selected from Out of the Hurly Burly:

> "Four doctors tackled Johnny Smith—
>   They blistered and they bled him;
> With squills and anti-bilious pills
>   And ipecac they fed him.

> "They stirred him up with calomel
>   And tried to move his liver;
> But all in vain—his little soul
>   Was wafted o'er the river."

Of another little youngster, just departed, Max warbles:

"Little Alexander's dead;
    Jam him in a coffin;
    Don't have as good a chance
    For a funeral often.

"Rush his body right around
    To the cemetery,
    Drop him in the sepulchre
    With his uncle Jerry."

In another instance, Adeler gets off the following horrible concoction:

"Ol bury Bartholomew out in the woods,
    In a beautiful hole in the ground,   .
    Where the bumble-bees buzz and the woodpeckers sing,
    And the straddle-bugs tumble around;
    So that in winter, when the snow and the slush
    Have covered his last little bed,
    His brother Artemas can go out with Jane
    And visit the place with his sled."

Then, I am pleased to give another choice selection from Clark's wonderful storehouse:

"The death angel smote Alexander McGlue,
    And gave him protracted repose;
    He wore a checked shirt and number nine shoe,
    And he had a pink wart on his nose.

"No doubt he is happier dwelling in space
    Over there on the evergreen shore.
    His friends are informed that his funeral takes place
    Precisely at quarter past four."

The same volume contains an admirable bit of drollery in the following take-off on art criticism:

ART NEWS.

We have received from the eminent sculptor, Mr. Felix Mullins, of Wilmington, a comic *bas relief,* designed for an ornamental fireboard. It represents an Irishman in his night-shirt running away with the little god Cupid, while the Irishman's sweetheart demurely hangs her head in the corner. Every true work of art tells its own story; and we understand, as soon as we glance at this, that our Irish friend has been coquetted with by the fair one, and is pretending to transfer his love to other quarters. There is a lurking smile on the Irishman's lips, which expresses his mischievous intentions perfectly. We think it would have been better to have clothed him in something else than a night-shirt, and to have smoothed down his hair. We have placed this *chef d' œuvre* upon a shelf in our office, where it will undoubtedly be admired by our friends when they call. We are glad to encourage such progress in Delaware art.

———

Adeler has given the public an admirable satire in his

IMPROVED CONGRESSIONAL RECORD.

If Congress resolve to act upon the suggestion of Senator Miller that the Congressional Record be issued as a weekly and sent to every family in the country, some modification ought to be made in the contents of the Record. The paper is much too heavy and dismal in its present condition to be welcomed in the ordinary American household. Perhaps it might have a puzzle department, and if so one of the first puzzles could take the shape of an inquiry how it happens that so many Congressmen get rich on a salary of five thousand a year. The department of answers to correspondents could be enriched with references to letters from office seekers, and the department of Household Economy could contain explanations of how the members frank their shirts home through the post-office so as to get them in the family wash. As for the general contents, describing the business proceedings in the Senate and the House, we recommend that these should be put in the form of verse. We should treat them, say, something in this fashion:

> Mr. Hill
> Introduced a bill
> To give John Smith a pension;
> Mr. Bayard
> Talked himself tired,
> But said nothing worthy of mention.   .

This would be succinct, musical, and a degree impressive. The youngest reader could grasp the meaning of it, and it could be easily committed to memory. Or a scene in the House might be depicted in such terms as these:

> A very able speech was made by Cox, of Minnesota,
> Respecting the necessity of protecting the black voter,
> 'Twas indignantly responded to by Smith, of Alabama,

Whose abominable talk was silenced by the Speaker's hammer.
Then Atkinson, of Kansas, rose to make an explanation,
But was pulled down by a colleague in a state of indignation.
And Mr. Alexander, in a speech about insurance,
Taxed the patience of his hearers pretty nearly past endurance,
After which Judge Whittaker denounced the reciprocity
Treaty with Hawaii as a scandalous monstrosity.

    *   *   *   *   *   *

Of course versification of the Congressional Record would require the services of a poet laureate of rather unusual powers. If Congress shall accept seriously the suggestions which we make with an earnest desire to promote the public interest, we shall venture to recommend the selection of the Sweet Singer of Michigan as the first occupant of the laureate's office."

CHARLES B. LEWIS.

The Detroit Weekly Free Press is a famous American newspaper. For a decade it has amused and instructed a hundred thousand families in the United States and Canada, yet prior to 1870 the paper was almost unknown outside the ·limits of the City of the Straits. The humorous column of the Free Press and the witty descriptive articles printed over the signature of " M. Quad," explains the secret of the success of this popular Detroit newspaper.

Charles B. Lewis, who is the proprietor of that typographical *nom de plume* " M. Quad," began writing for the Free Press as far back as 1870, and since that time the success of the paper has been almost phenomenal. The Detroit Free Press has not only attained an immense circulation in this country, but has carried its success across the Atlantic, where in the great English metropolis a weekly edition of the Detroit Free Press is issued for the amusement and gratification of all English-reading Europe.

The life of M. Quad has been a most romantic one, and if properly told would fill a volume. He is now over fifty years of age, and is a native of East Liverpool, Ohio. At the early age of fourteen, Lewis became "printers' devil" in the office of the Lansing (Michigan) Journal. At the breaking out of the war he enlisted in a Michigan regiment and served both in cavalry and infantry, winning many laurels on the field of battle. After the war he went West and tried Indian fighting for a time. Winning a lieutenantcy he retired and entered journalism. In 1868 he came near being killed by being blown up on the steamer Magnolia, on the Ohio river. When he came down he was dragged out on the shore by an old woman, who laid him out unconscious, among the dead and wounded on the beach. He was taken for a dead negro and was carted away to the morgue for burial.

He revived after a time, his wounds were dressed and he recovered in a few days. Afterwards he wrote a humorous account of the explosion, which was in a vein so irresistibly funny that it started him on the road to fame. In 1870 he finally settled down as a humorous writer on the Detroit Free Press, with which journal he has been connected ever since.

Lewis published Goaks and Tears in 1875,

which he prefaced by a ''a brief biography of M.
Quad, the Free Press man, written by his mother-
in-law." In this production he says of himself:

BIOGRAPHY OF M. QUAD.

There was nothing remarkable about his baby-
hood except his red hair and the great quantity of
soothing syrup necessary to keep him toned
down.

He was born of humble parents. His father
had never been on a jury, delivered a Fourth of
July oration, or been sued for slander, and his
mother had never rescued anybody from drown-
ing, or delivered a lecture on woman's rights.

He never had any brothers or sisters. He
might have had in due time, but his midnight
howls wore his mother out when he was two years
old, and she went to join the angels and left him
to howl it out.

His father was accidentally shot while courting
a second wife, and the boy kicked the clothes off
the bed to find himself an orphan.

He was the sole heir to all the property, and
the property consisted of a wheelbarrow, a tooth-
brush, and one or two other things. The boy's
uncle swooped down on the estate, stole every
thing but the debt it was owing, and the orphan
was given a grand bounce into the cold and heart-
less world.

But little is known of his boyhood.   He probably had patches before and behind, like other
orphans ; wept over the grave of his mother in his
sad moments, and crawled under the circus canvas
in his hours of sunshine.   Nothing in his demeanor
attracted the attention of John Jacob Astor or
Commodore Vanderbilt, and consequently he had
more cuffs than fat clerkships.

At the age of fifteen he was invited to go up
in a balloon.

He didn't go.

When he was seventeen he decided to become
a pirate, and all the captains of the Erie canal dis-
couraged him.

At eighteen he was in the legislature—sat there
and heard a speech and then left with the other
spectators.

At twenty he was foreman of a fire company,
but was impeached because he couldn't " holler "
as loudly as " No. 7."

He had just reached his majority when he led a
rich and beautiful girl to the altar—and handed
her over to the bridegroom.   He commenced in
that year to be a "head-writer" on newspapers.
Was almost daily informed that his proper sphere
was acting governor of a state, or in commanding
armies, but he stuck to journalistic work.

He was funny from the start, but it took eighteen years to make people believe it. He has had many wives, and is the father of scores of happy children. He has had the cholera and small-pox, written articles varying from astronomy to the best manner of curing hams, been wrecked, shot, assassinated, and banished, and is to-day hale, hearty, and bald-headed.

All reports about a steamboat blowing him up are canards. He blew the boat up.

For further particulars see circulars.

For ten years after M. Quad joined forces with the Detroit Free Press he wrote steadily for that journal, and rarely allowed an issue of the paper to be made without a humorous article from his pen. Since 1880, however, little or no humor has appeared, Mr. Lewis changing suddenly from a gay, rollicking style to descriptive sketches, thoughtful and pathetic. In 1881 he made a lengthy visit to the South and tramped over the old battlefields of the Rebellion. In the columns of the Free Press he described, in a series of weekly letters, the battles and the battlefields of the engagements with which he had been connected during the war. These letters were written under the title of Sixteen Years After, and signed by M. Quad. They have been copied extensively by the American and foreign press.

One of the raciest things that has ever appeared from the pen of Charles B. Lewis, is the following:

NEW YEAR'S ADDRESS.

Once more the whirligig of time has yanked an old year out, and a new one in.

Glad on't.

If there is anything lonesome and monotonous, it is last year. The old year had a few charms, but the new one promises to give them half a mile the start, and then go under the string first.

And yet one feels a trifle sad to part with the old year, when he comes to think it over. As memory's bob-tail car pulls us down the long lane of the past, one looks out of the window at the well-remembered objects of former days, and his heart saddens.

Where's the fat girl who rested her head on your bosom when the old year was new? Gone—yes, gone—slid out to take charge of the snake-cage in a traveling museum of natural wonders, and your wounded heart sorrowfully but vainly calls,—

"Come back, fat girl—come back?"

Where's the alligator boots which sat around the festive board last new year's day? Where's the silk umbrella you left on the doorstep this morning?

Where's the ton of coal and the jar of country

butter you laid in about that time? Where's the plumber who agreed to "come right up," and thaw that water-pipe out? The sad wind sighing through the treeless leaves, solemnly puckers its mouth, and sadly answers,—

"Gone up!"

One by one they have fallen beside the curb-stone of life's dreary highway, have been swept over and almost forgotten, while you and I have been spared to put up the stoves another time, and to have the landlord raise the rent on us—drat him! It makes one feel sad, especially the rent business.

Farewell, old year! If you go west to grow up with the country, or go south to run a steamboat, we hope you'll be honest, seek respectable com-pany, and make your daily life a striking example for, and a terrible warning to, the man who goes around playing the string game on unsuspecting people.

Welcome, new year! Howdy? If convenient, give us some new clothes, a few thousand in cash, and a race-horse, and prove by your actions that you mean to do the right thing by a fellow. Give us some strawberry weather this month, wollop the pesky Indians into behaving themselves, and make it uncomfortable for grasshoppers and potato-bugs. Be around with some decent weather when a fellow wants to go fishing, and let 'er rain to kill when the women go out to exhibit their new bonnets.   Do the fair thing by all of us, including New Jersey, and we won't stand by and see you abused.

HENRY W. SHAW.

"Josh Billings," the far-famed writer of Yankee proverbs, is over sixty years of age, yet hale and rather hearty. He was born in western Massachusetts, and after having a hard time of it in life, working at various times, in various places, in various states, at various occupations, he finally settled down to the peace and quiet of an author, with an occasional lecturing tour. This has been the life history of Henry W. Shaw, whose eccentric mode of spelling has made him famous. His eccentricities are not assumed and artificial, but a part of the man, and in his daily conversations he uses the same apt and peculiar similies that are characteristic of his pen productions.

In 1872, when asked by a friend to give some facts relative to his life, Josh wrote the following biography, which is very characteristic of the man:

"I was born in Berkshire county, Massachusetts, during the nineteenth century, of highly respectable parents, and owe what little success I have obtained to the wisdom of my father and the piety of my mother. At the fragrant age of fifteen I set my face westward and followed it until I stood on the banks of the wide Missouri, without any plans for life, and but little better in feelings than a cheerful vagrant. For twenty-five years the various wanderings of a border life made me acquainted with scenes and experiences better calculated to cut the character sharp, than to refine it, and if I escaped without scars, it was simply because the susceptibility of my nature looked upon most things in this life as simply a joke.

"In common with most all Americans who have to push early, to test their own wings, I engaged in all the usual enterprises of a frontiersman, having been at times a land hunter, farmer, drover, steamboat captain, auctioneer, politician, and even pioneer, for I partially organized an enterprise, as early as 1835, to cross the Rocky mountains. This last named enterprise was a profound failure, but its inception and preliminary arrangements afforded me one of the choicest relics of my early adventures, and that in *three letters*, now in my possession, written to me personally by Henry Clay, John Quincy Adams, and Martin Van Buren, recommending me and the undertaking to the kind care and patronage of all people and all nations.

" If I may be said to ever have commenced a literary career it certainly was much later in life than most men commit the folly, for I had passed forty-five years before I ever wrote a line for the publick eye. What little reputation I may have made, has been accomplished within the last nine years, and I consider that I owe all this little to the kindness of the world at large, who, while they have discovered but little wit, or even humor, in what I have written, have done me the credit to acknowledge that my productions have been free from malice. I pin all my faith, hope, and charity upon this one impulse of my nature, and that is, if I could have my way, there would be a smile continually on the face of every human being on God's footstool, and this smile should ever and anon widen into a broad grin.

" I have not the inclination to go into an extended account of the trials and failures that I have met with since I first put on the cap and bells, but I can assure you that I would not contend with them again for what little glory and stamps they have won for me. I have written two books, but my pet is Josh Billings' Farmer's Almanac, which has been issued for the last three years, the annual sale of which has exceeded one hundred thousand copies. This little waif will soon make its appearance for 1873, and I hope to make it a welcome guest for many years to come.

"My lectures, if they can be called lectures, are three in number, rejoicing under the very familiar titles of Milk, What I Know About Hotels, and the Pensive Cockroach. In this last discourse, a large invoice of reptiles, beasts, and fishes are handled, without mercy, commencing with the dreamy cockroach and touching lightly at times the cunning of the fox, the strange uncertainty of the flea, and the wondrous hypocracy of the cat.

"Please excuse, my dear sirs, in this hasty sketch what may appear not to be true, for he who writes about himself is in great danger of telling too much, or too little. My only apology for this monograph is, that it has been written at your request.

"Yours calmly,

JOSH BILLINGS."

———

Mr. Shaw began writing for the literary weeklies, and even now writes a half column or so of his quaint paragraphs for the New York Weekly. His almanac and other books have been published through the house of George W. Carleton, New York, and have had a wonderful sale. It is said that Josh has made at least $100,000 by his writ-

ings.   It has been stated that his uncouth manner
of spelling was adopted, in the first instance, quite
as much through fear of his ability to spell cor-
rectly, as through the wish to be odd.   He avoided
criticism by intentional· and habitual misspelling.
He is by nature a philosopher, and the experiences
of his whole life are classified in his mind, as illus-
trations of this or that quality of human nature.

Soon after he became famous in the walks of
literature, Shaw entered the lecture field.   He became at once very popular, and drew large and
cultured audiences in the East and West.   His
last lecturing tour of any length proved very
profitable to him.   He lectured on The Probabilities of Life, which was divided, as he says, into
twenty-four chapters.   The hand-bills announcing
this lecture read as follows :

"Josh Billings will deliver his new, and as he
calls it, serio-comic lecture, on 'The Probabilities
of Life' (perhaps rain, perhaps not).   Divided
into twenty-four cantos, as follows :   A Genial
Overture of Remarks ; the Long Branch Letter ;
Human Happiness as an Alternative ; the Live
Man, a Busy Disciple ; a Second Wife, a Good
Risk to Take ; the Poodle with Azure Eyes ; the
Handsome Man, a Failure ; Short Sentences, Sharp
at Both Ends ; the Fastidious Person, Fuss and
Feathers ; Patience, Slow Poison ; What I Know

about Hotels, a Sad History ; the Flea, a Brisk
Package ; the Domestic Man, a Necessary Evil ;
Answers to Correspondents ; Jonah and his Whale ;
Marriage, a Draw Game ; Mary Ann, a Modest
Maiden ; the Mother-in-law, one of the Luxuries ;
Proverbs, Truth on the Half Shell ; the Mouse, a
Household Hord ; the Life Insurance Agent ; the
Caterpillar, a Slow Bug ; the First Baby, too
Sweet for Anything ; Sayings of a promiscuous
nature.   And much other things."

Shaw's advertising dodges have all been of a
funny and striking character.   The following lines
appeared on a postal card that was sent broadcast
during the winter of 1877 :

' Josh Billings and the Young Man.   Young
man, don't kry for spilt milk, but pik up yure pail
and milking stool, and go for the next cow.
Yures affekshionately, Josh Billings.   For sale or
To Let.   Price Neat, But Not Gaudy.   Contem-
plating a trip to California during the winter of
1877, I will read my old and venerable lecture,
' MILK,' before any association who may desire
to hear it.   The ' Milk ' in this lecture is con-
densed, and will keep sweet in any climate.

"Your cheerful friend,

JOSH BILLINGS."

Josh is getting old, and each succeeding year
his literary productions are fewer and shorter.

Out of the fortune he has made by his pen, only $50,000 is retained in his possession. He is an odd-looking genius, tall, stoop-shouldered, with a large head, massive face, deep-set eyes, and grizzly beard. His hair, which was formerly brown, is now an iron gray, and his stiff, drooping mous-tache is fast changing to the same color. He parts his hair in the middle, combs it smoothly behind his ears, allowing it to fall loosely on his neck like the locks of a school-girl.

A newspaper writer, in speaking of Josh not long since, said : "As he grows older, he seems to become more and more supremely regardless of persons, surroundings, or opinions. As he greets one with the machine like 'How do ye do,' or an inanimate 'Good day,' the impression is conveyed that he has arrived at the state of life and prosperity where he deems fate powerless to work any alteration for the worse. Billings is essentially a man to himself, taciturn and unob-trusive everywhere. He is now a willing but unat-tractive lecturer. He and his wife pass a quiet, relegated, but doubtless contented life, in an unpretentious dwelling in Sixty-third street, New York city, the garret of which is made to answer the combined purpose of literary sanctum and storehouse."

Shaw has written many witty things besides his

quaint "Proverbs," which made him famous. The following is an example:

THE HEIGHT OF SUBLIMITY.
AN ADVERTISEMENT BY JOSH BILLINGS.

I kan sell for eighteen hundred and thirty-nine dollars, a pallas, a sweet and pensive retirement, located on the virgin banks of the Hudson, kontaining 85 acres. The land is luxuriously divided by the hand of natur and art, into pastor and tillage, into plain and deklivity, into stern abruptness and the dallianse ov moss-tufted medder; streams of sparkling gladness (thick with trout) danse through this wilderness of buty, tow the low musik of the kricket and grasshopper. The evergreen sighs az the evening zephir flits through its shadowy buzzum, and the aspen trembles like the love-smitten hart of a damsell. Fruits of the tropicks, in golden buty, melt on the bows, and the bees go heavy and sweet from the fields to their garnering hives. The stables are worthy of the steeds of Nimrod or the studs of Akilles, and its henery was bilt expressly for the birds of paradice; while somber in the distance, like the cave of a hermit, glimpses are caught ov the dog-house. Here poets have come and warbled their laze, here sculpters have cut, here painters hav robbed the scene of dreamy landskapes, and here the philosopher diskovered the stun which made him the alkimist ov natur. As the young moon hangs like a curting ov silver from the blue breast of the ski, an angel may be seen each night dansing with golden tip-toes on the grass. (N. B.—The angel goes with the place.)

———

To show what Josh's Proverbs are like, I annex a few as a finale to this sketch :

PROVERBS.

Thare haz been menny a hero born, lived and died unknown, just for the want ov an opportunity.

Thare ain't nothing that will sho the virtues and vices of a man in so vivid a light as profuse prosperity.

It is a good deal ov a bore to have others luv us more than we luv them.

Mi dear boy, allwuss keep sumthing in reserve. The man who can jump six inches further than he ever haz jumpt, iz a hard customer to beat.

Thare ain't nothing on arth that will take the starch so klean out ov us, as to git kaught bi the phellow we are trying to ketch.

JAY CHARLTON GOLDSMITH.

Thirty-eight or forty years ago, Jay Charlton Goldsmith, of the New York Herald, was ushered into the world with little if any ceremony. He was born in a small village in eastern New York, not far from the great metropolis. Like other dutiful sons, Jay pleased his parents by attending school until he was thirteen years of age. He then entered a lawyer's office and mingled with his legal learning the study of phonography. About this time he began acting as correspondent for the Herald from the rural district wherein he lived. At the age of sixteen he was one of the editors of the Register, a small evening paper published at Patterson, New Jersey.

The health of the young man, however, forbade his steady working in a newspaper office, and a year later he was compelled to relinquish his position. He immediately began preparations for a journey abroad, his intention being to travel two years on the continent. He changed his mind at the last moment and went to California, and from there to the Sandwich Islands. During these travels he penned very creditable and quite readable letters to the Herald. He also wrote occasionally for other journals. On his return, after an absence of a year, he accepted an editorial position in the office of the Republican, at Savannah, Georgia. His health again failing him, he was driven from the South by the climate.

In 1867 he returned to New York city, where he became a reporter and occasional editorial writer for the Tribune. When Oakey Hall became mayor of New York, Goldsmith, who was a warm personal friend, became his private secretary. He retained this office for four years. Early in 1873 he succeeded Mr. E. G. Squier as editor of Frank Leslie's Illustrated Newspaper. While editing this journal he wrote many critical, terse articles, which attracted general attention. His health again failing, he made a second visit to the Pacific coast two years later. About this time Goldsmith commenced writing to the Danbury News, a series of letters signed by "Jay Charlton," which became a feature of that famous publication.

Five or six years later, finding himself greatly improved in health, he again accepted a situation on the New York Herald, and has retained it ever since. One of his duties was to write the Personal Intelligence column. He determined to

make it spicy, and wrote short items that could
be read between bites at the breakfast table. The
name of the "P. I. Man," by which Goldsmith is
so widely known, was probably derived from this
fact.

He is said to be the editor of the Weekly Herald, and adds much to the character and worth of
that popular edition of Bennett's famous newspaper. Goldsmith is an odd looking, but not
unhandsome genius. He wears his black hair
long and it hangs down upon his neck and forehead in profusion. He possesses a poetic face,
which is adorned with heavy side-whiskers.

Jay Charlton's Hints to Farmers is one of his
best efforts. It shows what horrible puns he
is capable of:

HINTS TO FARMERS.

Early Rose potatoes should be planted early.
It is not called Early because it grows on rose
bushes, but because it gets up at five o'clock in
the morning. Do not make the mistake of peeling
these potatoes before planting. The potato is to
be eaten whole. Mashed potatoes should be sown
broadcast.

The string bean is the best bean for growing on
strings. One string will do for ten beans. Some
of the high strung beans need poles. These may be
pulled up and taken on fishing excursions, and be

returned with the line attached. The best strings for these beans are B strings.

The Champion of England peas were named after Tom Sayers, the great prize fighter. These peas do not need any pods on them. We have planted them for many years without pods on them. One great advantage of the Champion of England peas is that they spar for themselves. Tom Sayers got away with two quarts of them once, but he trusted too much to his own ability. You cannot handle the Champion of England without gloves. In selecting ground for them it is best to have the sun in their eyes. They can stand a good deal of rough weather, but have been known to yield to a knock-down blow. Peas should never be eaten with a knife, because they roll off. It is best to pour them into a funnel.

Oats should not be planted wild. Still we have known oats sown wild to produce a larger crop than the tame oats. Many of them are sown by moonlight and some by gas-light, but it is sometimes worse for the man who raises them than for the oats themselves. The best place to sow oats is in doors by a nice fire, and with a little sprinkling of cold water. Whiskey is a destroyer of the crop, and although very good for harrowing in, induces a growth of weeds. In Scotland the oats are fed to men, and in England to horses; so that a famous Scotchman said that nowhere could such horses be found in the world as in England, and nowhere such men as in Scotland. This is the reason why, on the borders, inns are sometimes called oatells. Oats are very heating, and many a Scotchman who eats them is compelled to come up to the scratch. Thus arises also that famous expression "hot Scotch," which refers to a Highlander who has had too many oats. They warm him up.

Do not fail to raise sheep. The proportion should be three dogs to one sheep. They will make it lively for the sheep. When you go woolgathering take your dinner with you, for you may get lost. Lambs are best cooked a lamb mode. Chinamen eat rice with mutton. Hence their knives and forks are called chop sticks. Thus a Chinaman will say, "Lamby hard to bleat." Lambs are best when they begin to gamble—you bet—on the green. It is funny, but Lamb's finest work was on pigs. Yet, *vice versa*, we have seen pigs getting in their best work on lamb and peas.

WILLIAM TAPPAN THOMPSON.

The subject of this sketch, although one of the oldest of American humorists, is comparatively unknown at the present time. William Tappan Thompson was born in the village of Ravenna, Portage county, Ohio, on the 31st day of August, 1812. He came from a good family, his father being a native of Virginia, and his mother the daughter of an Irish exile. At the age of twelve years young Thompson' was an orphan, and was thrown upon his own resources in the city of Philadelphia. He entered the office of the Philadelphia Chronicle, where he remained for two years working as a printer's apprentice.

At the age of eighteen he left his newly found occupation and went to Florida with Acting-Governor Wescott as his private secretary. About the same time he began the study of law. In 1835, he was at work again as a printer, in the office of the Sentinel at Augusta, Georgia. Later on in the same year he became a volunteer with

the Richmond Blues and served for nearly two
years in the Seminole war.

Late in the autumn of 1836 Mr. Thompson
issued the first number of the Augusta Mirror,
but it proved a dismal failure.   It was during the
Mirror trouble that the young editor became the
duly wedded husband of a daughter of Joseph
Carrie, a well-to-do merchant of Barnwell, South
Carolina, and Augusta, Georgia.   After the death
of the Mirror, Mr. Thompson took editorial charge
of the Madison Miscellany, and it was his writings
for this journal that in after years made him famous
as a humorist.

During his idle moments Mr. Thompson began
a series of letters from '' Major Joseph Jones of
Pineville.'' These were begun in 1842, and became
very popular—so much so, in fact, that before a
year had elapsed after their first appearance, they
were collected in a volume and published under
the title of Major Jones' Courtship.   In the preface of the book the author dedicated the work to
his old commander in the Seminole war, General
Duncan L. Clinch.

Edition after edition of the book was issued,
and it was known in every city and town on this
side of the Atlantic.   Later, it was reprinted in
London, where it had an enormous run for several
years.   A recent writer in a New Haven paper

says of Major Jones' Courtship: "Its style is rollicking without grossness; piquant, yet devoid of all exaggeration.   Re-reading these letters to-day, the freshness and vigor, which so charmed my youthful fancy for the grotesque in home life, are reflected from every page."

The preface of the book was written April 10, 1843, and among other things contains the following: "It's a great deal easier to write a heap of nonsense than it is to put a good face on it after its rit—and I don't know when I've had a job that puzzled me so much how to begin it.   I've looked over a whole heap of books to see how other writers done, but they all seemed to be about the same thing.   They all feel a monstrous desire to benefit the public one way or other; some is anxious to tell all they know about certain matters, just for the good of the public, some has been swaded by friends to give the book to the public, and others have been induced to publish their ritens just for the benefit of future generations,—but not one of 'em ever had an idea to make a cent for themselves!   Now, none of these excuses don't zactly meet my case.   I don't spose the public—cept it is them as is courtin—will be much benefited by readin my letters—I'm sure Mr. Thompson wouldn't went to all the expense just to please his friends, and for my part I'm perfectly willin to let posterity write their own books. So I don't see any other way than to jest come rite out with the naked truth—and that is, that *my book was made just a purpose to sell and make money.* Ther ain't a single lie in the book, and I'm termined ther sha'n't be none in the preface.

"I hain't got no very grate opinion of myself, but I've always tried to live honest, and what little character I is got I want to keep. When Mr. Thompson just writ me word, he was gwine to put my letters in a book, I felt sort o' skeered, for fear them bominable criticks might take hold of it, and tare it all to flinders—as they always nabs a'most every thing that's got a kiver on ; but, when I come to think, there were two ways of gettin into the field—under and over the fence. Well, the criticks is like a pretty considerable high fence round the public taste; and books get into the world of letters jest as a boy does in a pertater patch—some over, and some under. Now and then one gets hung, and the way it gets peppered is distressin—but them that gets in under the fence is jest as safe as them that gits in over. Seein as I is perfectly satisfied with the under route, I don't think the criticks will tackle my book—if they does, all I can say is, I give 'em joy with their small potaters."

After the success of Major Jones' Courtship,

Mr. Thompson issued other works from time to time. Major Jones' Sketches of Travel appeared a few years later, and was' followed by The Chronicles of Pineville. Mr. Thompson also wrote a farce entitled, The Live Indian, and a dramatization of The Vicar of Wakefield. Messrs. Carey & Hart, of Philadelphia, bought the copyright of Major Jones' Courtship in 1848, for the paltry sum of $250. In 1856 Mr. Thompson prepared for the press, Hotchkiss' Codification of the Statute Laws of Georgia, and in 1858 became connected with the Western Continent, a weekly illustrated paper published in Baltimore.

Two years later he sold his interest in the Western Continent, and went to Savannah, where, in company with John M. Cooper, he issued the Savannah Morning News, which is now valuable newspaper property. During the Rebellion Mr. Thompson was appointed aid to Governor Brown, which position he held until the fall of Savannah. In 1877 he was a member of the Georgia Constitutional convention, which is the full extent of his political career. For the past thirty years he has been the editor of the Morning News, and has been one of the leading citizens of Savannah. His work at present is the superintendency and the occasional writing of editorials for his newspaper.

It is many years since he gave to the world a specimen of his old-time humor.

Since writing the above, I have been pained to learn of the sudden death of Mr. Thompson, at his home in Savannah, on the 24th day of March, 1882.   His death revives the subject of his works, and his several books are to be republished in Philadelphia at an early date.

MELVILLE D. LANDON.

Eli Perkins is a name well known to Americans. In fact he is so well known that sundry newspaper writers, who should feel heartily ashamed of themselves for so doing, have classed Eli Perkins with Gath, Private Dalzell, George Francis Train, and other equally noted characters. The same sundry newspaper writers have stated at various times that Eli Perkins was the greatest liar in all America. This is a base falsehood, and an attack upon the name of a honorable gentleman. A liar, indeed! If the humorists of America are to be thus defiled simply because they exaggerate good stories, solely for the purpose of displaying their wit, why the occupation of humorist is valueless.

Melville D. Landon, better known as Eli Perkins, is not only a humorist, but is author, lecturer, and journalist as well. He was born in Eaton, Madison county, New York, in the year 1840. His freshman year was passed at Madison university, and in 1861 he graduated from Union col-

lege under Dr. Nott, and two years later he received the honorary degree of Master of Arts.
He entered journalism soon after this, and after
several years of hard work he went to Europe
and Asia, returning in 1868.

Eli Perkins was by nature a humorist, yet he
devoted himself at first entirely to serious writings.
In 1871 he issued his first book from the press of
George W. Carleton, New York. It was a large
volume of over six hundred pages, and was a de-
tailed history of the Franco-Prussian war. It was
a book solemn as the grave, yet full of thrilling
description. It commanded a large and ready
sale.

An old friend tells the following interesting anec-
dote of Mr. Landon at this time : "In 1872, at
the age of thirty-three, a great change came over
Mr. Landon. It was then for the first time that
he unchecked his pen, and allowed fun and humor
to creep unobstructed into his writings. The
occasion was a series of letters written from Saratoga, since republished in Saratoga in 1901.
These letters were written for the New York Commercial Advertiser, at the instance of Hugh J.
Hastings, a veteran, fun-loving journalist. The
Commercial was then almost a dead newspaper.
It was never seen on the news-stands, and was
only taken in a few old families, who still stuck to

the paper because of its antiquity, it having been established in 1794.

"Perkins appeared one day at the leading news-stand in Saratoga, and marching up with great pride, informed the newsman that he was going to write for the Commercial.

"'For the Co— what?" asked the man.

"'For the Co-mercial—the Commercial Advertiser."

"'Never heard of it, sir," replied the newsman.

"'Well, I am going to write for it, and I want you to order it."

"'No use, can't sell it sir, and——'

"'But I'll buy it—buy all you have left," expostulated Eli.

"'All right,' said the newsman, 'then I'll order five copies.'

"Every day after that these letters were published in the Commercial under the signature of Eli Perkins. They set Saratoga on fire. The demand for them was immense. On the street cars in New York, and on the balconies in Saratoga, people were reading the letters and asking 'Who is Eli Perkins?' In four weeks after the humorist commenced writing six hundred copies of the Commercial were sold in Saratoga alone.

"In a word, the articles made Eli Perkins famous. They were widely read and copied, and many of them were reproduced in France and Spain. Perkins and Mark Twain were the only humorists at that time since the death of Artemus Ward, and it was no wonder that there was a demand for their writings."

A few years later the Saratoga letters were gathered together, illustrated by Arthur Lumley, and republished in a large volume by Sheldon & Co., of New York. Still later Mr. Landon issued another book—a volume of humorous sketches—entitled Eli Perkins at Large. This production had, and yet has, an immense sale. In 1872, he entered the lecture field, and for eight or ten years he has convulsed hundreds of audiences in every part of the country, North, East, South, and West. He has also kept up his literary work, and has been corresponding regularly for the Chicago Tribune. His letters to this well known journal have been widely copied and are noted for their sparkling wit and rollicking humor.

Eli produced something intensely funny when he wrote

ELI PERKINS ON AMERICAN BULLS.

Punctuation makes a great many bulls in this country. The other day I picked up a newspaper in Wisconsin full of curious things. I enclose a few specimens:

"The procession at Judge Orton's funeral was

very fine and nearly two miles in length as was the beautiful prayer of the Rev. Dr. Swing from Chicago."

Another:

"A cow was struck by lightning on Saturday belonging to Dr. Hammond who had a beautiful spotted calf only four days old."

A distressing accident is thus chronicled:

"A sad accident happened to the family of John Elderkin on Main street, yesterday. One of his children was run over by a market wagon three years old with sore eyes and pantalets on that never spoke afterwards."

The next morning after lecturing at Jonesville, I saw this paragraph:

"George Peck, an intemperate editor from Milwaukee fell over the gallery last night while Eli Perkins was lecturing in a beastly state of intoxication.

"The coroner's jury brought in a verdict that Mr. Peck came to his death by remaining too long in a cramped position while listening to Mr. Perkins' lecture which produced apoplexy on the minds of the jury."

CHARLES FOLLEN ADAMS.

Some years ago, a poem in broken German verse, overflowing with the richest of humor, appeared in a Boston paper. It was entitled Leedle Yawcob Strauss, and commanded general attention immediately upon its publication. It was copied widely and was sent on its way across the ocean, delighting hundreds on the other side of the Atlantic. The poem ran thus :

> " I haf von funny leedle poy,
>   Vot gomes schust to my knee;
> Der queerest schap, der createst roke
>   As efer you did see ;
> He runs, and schumps, und schmashes dings
>   In all barts off der house—
> But vot off dot? He vas mine son,
>   Mine leedle Yawcob Strauss.
>
> " He gets der measles und der mumbs,
>   Und eferyding dot's out ;
> He sbills mine glass of lager pier,
>   Poots schnuff into mine kraut ;
> He fills mine pipe mit Limburg cheese—
>   Dot vas der roughest chouse ;
> I'd take dot vrom no oder poy
>   But leedle Yawcob Strauss.

" He dakes der milk ban for a dhrum,
   Und cuts mine cane in dwo,
To make der shtick to beat it mit—
   Mine cracious, dot vas drue !
I dinks mine head vas schplit about
   He kicks up such a touse?
But nefer mind, der poys vas few
   Like dot young Yawcob Strauss.

" He asks me questions sooch as dese :
   Who baints mine nose so red ?
Who vas it cuts dot schmoodt blace oudt
   Vrom the hair ubpon mine hed ?
Und vhere der plaze goes vrom der lamp
   Vene'er der glim I douse ?
How gan I all dese dings eggsplain
   To dot schmall Yawcob Strauss ?

" I somedimes dink I schall go vild
   Mit sooch a grazy poy,
Und vish vonce more I gould haf rest
   Und beaceful dimes enshoy ;
But ven he vas ashleep in ped,
   So quiet as a mouse,
I prays der Lord, ' Dake anydings,
   But leaf dot Yawcob Strauss.' "

When in later years another poem, "Dot Leedle Loweeza," a companion piece to ''Leedle Yawcob Strauss,'' appeared, the fame of the author, Charles Follen Adams, rose still higher. '' Dot Leedle Loweeza '' was equally as good as its predecessor, and concluded as follows :

''Vhen winter vas come, midst its coldt, shtormy veddher,
   Katrina und I musd sit in der house
Und dalk of der bast, by der fireside togedder,
   Or blay mit dat taughter of our Yawcob Strauss.
Oldt age, mit its wrinkles, pegins to remind us

Ve gannot shtay long mit our children to dwell ;
Budt soon ve shall meet, mit der poys left behind us,
Und dot shweet Loweeza, dot lofe us so well."

There are many other poems that have been written by Mr. Adams in a manner similar to his first two efforts, which have attracted general attention. Charles Follen Adams does not follow the occupation of a journalist or literary man, but is a well known merchant of Boston. He is a genuine Yankee, and his parents come of good old Puritan stock. From his mother's side, he is a direct descendant from Hannah Dustan, famous in the history of the Deerfield massacre. He is a man of middle age and of small stature. A friend thus describes him : " He is a dapper little gentleman, neat and natty in his *personnel*, just as though he had stepped from a band box, a shrewd, sharp, yet kindly face, a keen, but bright and laughing eye, which tells of a fine sense of humor, a close shaven face, with the exception of a 'bald browed mustache,' which gives a manly tone to the well shaped mouth and rounded chin, of medium and slender physique, he steps off with a nervy, springy walk, and a sunny smile or a genial word for his many friends and acquaintances as he passes them on the way."

Mr. Adams lives happily with his family at No. 36 Rutland square, where he spends his leisure moments in writing for the press. He contributes regularly a column of bright, witty paragraphs in the Cambridge Tribune, and occasionally writes for the Detroit Free Press, and other publications. Once in a great while he drops into poetry for the magazines.

A collection of his poems was published in book form by a Boston house, a year or two ago, under the title of "Leedle Yawcob Strauss and Other Poems." The volume had an immense sale and is still very popular. Mr. Adams is engaged in the mercantile business on Hanover street, and will probably remain so connected with the business world for many years.

Mr. Adams does not confine his writings wholly to the German dialect. In a recent number of The Century he contributes some verses which he is pleased to call Prevalent Poetry.

> " A wandering tribe called the Sioux
> Wear moccasins, having no shioux.
>   They are made of buckskin
>   With the fleshy side in,
> Embroidered with beads of bright hyioux,

> " When out on the war path, the Sioux
> March single file—never by tioux—
>   And by blazing the trees
>   Can return at their ease
> And their way through the forest ne'er lioux."

After two more verses in a similar strain, Mr. Adams concludes as follows :

" Now doesn't this spelling look cyiouxrious ?
'Tis enough to make anyone byiouxrious !
So a word to the wise !
Pray our language revise
With orthography not so injiouxrious."

SEBA SMITH.

Before the close of the last century a famous humorist was born in the town of Buckfield, in the State of Maine. Seba Smith was his name, yet during his entire life few persons knew him by that title. Speaking of him as "Majer Jack Downing," however, instantly recalls him to mind, and he at once becomes well known.

Seba Smith was born on the 19th day of September, 1792. As early as 1818 he graduated from Bowdoin College, and, a year or two later, settled in Portland, where, in 1820, he became the editor of the Eastern Argus. In 1830 he transferred his labors to the Portland Courier, with which journal he was connected until 1837. It was during this time that Mr. Smith wrote a series of letters for his paper. They were of a political nature, and took well with the public. They became so popular that in 1833 they were collected in a volume and published in Boston, under the caption of Life and Letters of Majer Jack Downing. The letters were humorous in the extreme, and being written on prominent political subjects, they became widely popular.

In 1841, Smith issued, also through a Boston house, a poem of considerable length, entitled Powhattan. The next year the friends of Majer Jack Downing found him in New York city, where he became actively engaged in literary work. His writings continued to be popular, and his books were written in rapid succession. Away Down East, or Portraitures of Yankee Life, appeared in 1843, and in 1846, a book entitled Dewdrops of the Nineteenth Century was issued. This was followed by a work, New Elements of Geometry, and other books of a serious nature.

In 1859, towards the close of the year, Mr. Smith issued another volume of political humor, which he called My 30 Years Out of the Senate. This book had a wide reputation, and attained an immense sale. The "late unpleasantness" found Mr. Smith hard at work, although now an old man. In 1864, he issued a book entitled Majer Jack Downing of the Downingville Militia. An English edition of the work now lies before me. It was printed in Paternoster Row, London, and contains just thirty chapters. On the title page is the following:

"The constitution is a dimmycratic machine,

and its got to run as a dimmycratic machine, or it
won't run at all!"

One of the richest things in the book is "A.
Linkin's Proclamashin Concerning Majer Jack
Downing's Book." This excellent "take-off" on
a President's proclamation is dated Washington,
July 15, 1864, and is as follows:

"Whereas, my friend, Majer Jack Downing,
of the Downingville millisha, has issued a Book
of Letters, containing his views on public affairs,
the war, etc., etc.

"Now, therefore, I do hereby issue this, my
Proclamashin, enjoyning upon every loyal, as well
as disloyal, citizen, includin' loyal Leegers, Aboli-
tionists, Republikans, War Dimmycrats, Copper-
heads, Clay Banks, Charcoals, &c., to buy this
book and to read the same, under penalty of the
confiscation of all their property, includin' niggers
of every descripshin. Furthermore, all officers
under me, whether, civil, military, or otherwise,
are hereby ordered, under penalty of court mar-
shal, to purchase the said book and read it. This
order applies to all Postmasters and their Clerks
(who are also ordered to assist in the sale of the
book), to all Custom House officials, Provo-Mar-
shalls, to all Tax Collectors, Assessors, Recrute-
ing Officers, Runners, Brokers, Bounty Jumpers,

and espeshully to all Government Swindlers, Con-
tractors, Defaulters, &c., to all Furrin Ambassa-
dors, Ministers, Penitentiaries, male and female,
&c &c.   Further more, Generals Grant, Sherman
and all other Generals, including Ginneral Banks,
will see to it that the Majer's letters are widely
circulated in the armies, as the menny good stories
of mine, as well as of the Majer's, in the book,
will keep the sojers in good sperits.

" Further more, if eny disloyal editer shall pre-
sume to say enything against this book, or advise
eny person not to sell or circulate the same, or aid
or abet them in so doing, he shall at once be arrested and his paper stopped.

" Further, if any person, in order to avoid the
penalties mentioned above, shall borrow said book,
he shall, if it be proved, be fined $1000 in gold,
If there be no proof, he shall be sent to Fort La-
fayette.

" Finally every person perchasing a copy of the
Majer's Letter shall be exempt from the draft.
All others are at once to be seized and sent to the
front.

" Done, in this, my city of Washington, in the
fourth year of my reign.   A. LINKIN."

The thirty letters following are all dated Washington and give a humorous account of matters
political at the National capital at that time.

Miss Elizabeth Oakes, a well known writer, was married to Mr. Smith when she was sixteen years of age. She was born in Cumberland, Maine, in 1831, and was a noted novelist for upwards of twenty years. She has published in all something like fifteen different works. She issued, in 1851, a volume, Woman and Her Needs, which became quite popular.

Mr. Smith retired to private life at the close of the war, and died on the 29th of July, 1868, at his homestead in Patchogue, Rhode Island. His wife survived him and was living in North Carolina several years ago. She gave up writing ten years since.

WILL W. CLARK.

Natives of western Pennsylvania are familiar with
two very characteristic names, "Frisbee" and
"Gilhooley." A short, stout, rather good looking
young man of twenty-eight or more is the father
of both cognomens, and every grown up resident in
smoky Pittsburgh will tell you who he is. Will W.
Clark, the paragrapher of the Pittsburgh Leader,
does not enjoy a national reputation, although he
deserves it. His character sketches signed "Frisbee" and "Gilhooley" are choice tidbits of humor, while his "All Sorts" column in the Evening
Leader is rarely dry or out of humor.

Clark was born in Pittsburgh, and will probably
die there. He is married and is the happy parent
of three children. Although but six years in the
journalistic harness, Will is already an old hand at
the business and is an accomplished reporter. He
is a hard-working journalist, who looks ahead for
bread and butter rather than for fame.

His humor is peculiar, and I can give no better
example of it than a life of himself, written by
himself, for himself. It is as follows:

"MY DEAR CLEMENS:

"My biography is not a particularly interesting chapter, and is in fact the romance of a poor young man. Still I think I am a humorist. Away down in the innermost recesses of my system I feel I am a humorist, but by some unfortunate combination of circumstances the public has never tumbled to the fact, with the proper precision and accuracy; the public wouldn't tumble if a marble front would fall on it. That is probably the reason I am on the ragged edge of genteel poverty at the present time instead of rolling in luxury.

"I was born in the classic precincts of Hardscrabble, of poor and presumably honest parents. I took a fancy to literature from my mother, who was a Scotch-Irish woman, a great reader, and knew Burns by heart.

"The old man was an Englishman with a bald head and side whiskers, and had a faculty of accumulating money, a faculty, I regret to say, which is not hereditary in our family. He used to remark, with some of that fine humor which I possess to such an intense degree, that he came from Derbyshire, 'where they were strong in the arm and weak in the head.'

"The most striking evidence of weakness on his part was his presenting me with a watch, in consideration of which I was not to enter the army.

On this occasion I became apprised, for the first time, that I was a humorist, as I had no notion of going to the front. I think it is much better to be a miserable poltroon during a war than a one-legged organ-grinder after it.

"It is singular that as a boy I was a good deal like other boys. At school I was the teacher's pet. She liked me because I was pretty, and she noticed that budding genius which has developed so grandly since, but of which the public has failed to take proper cognizance. When I had reached decimals in arithmetic and could declaim 'Rolla's Address to the Peruvians,' the old man considered that my education was complete, and put me to work.

" He was a rough carpenter, and I became a rough carpenter. I think I was the roughest carpenter in the United States. I built a shed once that was constructed in a manner so diametrically opposite to all the rules of carpentry, that it caved in three days after its completion and killed two coal heavers. On another occasion my employer noticed that I put a lock on upside down and hung a door the wrong way. He kindly but firmly suggested that I should quit. After revolving the question in my own mind I did quit; I thought the employer would be angry if I didn't.

"When my father died he left me some money

and I was pretty well fixed, but in a moment of abberation of mind I yielded to the advice of some of my friends and joined a building and loan association. That settled it; in a short time the association gobbled my property and was loaning my money to some one else. If I had a hundred sons I would advise them all to be solicitors for or presidents of building and loan associations. There's money in it.

"After that I made the most gigantic mistake of my life. I got a job on a newspaper as a reporter, and, after stoving my legs up running a route, I bloomed out as a humorist writer. As I said before, the people don't know I'm a humorist, but that is due to their lack of appreciation, and is no fault of mine. I have written some of the most exquisitely all-but funny things I ever saw, and I am now engaged on a series of important jokes for an almanac. I have a wife, three children, and an occasional dose of dyspepsia.

"I do not intend to retire from business for some time. The newspaper business is easy, and especially easy is the task of running the funny end of it. A fellow has merely to be funny when he feels sad, and to grind out humorous items every day in the year. Then the salary of newspaper men is so enormous that college graduates would rather take a situation on a newspaper than get a job driving a street car. I am still grinding out mental pabulum for the public, and still waiting for some appreciative newspaper publisher to offer me a situation at $5,000 per annum.

W. W. CLARK."

IRWIN RUSSELL.

The night before Christmas, 1879, witnessed the death of one of the brightest young humorists the United States has ever called her own. Of bright intellect and finished education, Irwin Russell was rapidly winning a name in American literature, when taken ill, as the result of overwork ; he lingered a few days, and died Christmas Eve.

Little is known of the early days of Irwin Russell. He was born in Fort Gibson, and at an early age was left an orphan, relying on his own exertions for a livelihood. He studied law and began the practice of it in his native city, but, becoming enamored with the life of a Bohemian, he started for New Orleans in search of fame and fortune· He obtained employment at local writing in various newspaper offices, and finally found regular employment in the editorial rooms of the New Orleans Times. Then he left the South and turned up in New York city, where he struggled with fate for a time. His existence was a battle with necessity from the first. It seemed that he was born unlucky. Although his prospects were always fine, he never lived to establish himself permanently anywhere. Few men ever received so many buffets from the hand of fate.

Alone and friendless in New York, young and ambitious, yet weak and moneyless, success and he were strangers. The health of the poor boy failed him, and he would have died had he remained in New York. He shipped on board of a steamer bound for the gulf, and worked his way home—not home, for he had none, but to New Orleans, where he had, at least, a few friends among the journalists of that city. He returned to work upon the Times, and published some of the daintiest bits of dialect humor ever given to the public.

By a strange coincidence his last published lines were written upon the subject of his own grave. They appeared in the New Orleans Times, December 14th, just ten days before the author gave up the struggle with fate and died.

THE CEMETERY.

"I stand within this solemn place,
　　And think of days gone by—
I think of many an old-time face,
　　Here's where those faces lie,

"I think of when, what time God please,
　　The hour shall came to me,

That covered with the clay, like these,
My face shall masked be.

"No marble monument shall rise
Above that grave of mine—
No loving friends will wipe their eyes
When life I shall resign.

"But when I leave my life—have left
My every present care—
I'll find a home of care bereft;
My friends are living there.

The New Orleans Times, in speaking of Irwin Russell, after his death, said of him: "He was employed occasionally on this paper, and while so, wrote many a pretty little poem, and many a little catch which reveal an inner life, which hard lines hid from the view of the world. His fund of humor showed itself best in dialect writing, and some things he has written have already found permanent resting places in the compiled editions of American humorous verse."

For several years Irwin Russell was an interesting and valued contributor to Scribner's Monthly, and some of his poems have appeared since his death, in The Century. The productions were mostly of the negro dialect order, and occasionally they consisted of Irish sketches in verse. About the last thing published was an Irish dialect poem, entitled Larry's on the Force, which appeared in The Century. The poem tells in the

fourth verse of Larry's appearance as a police-
man:

" He shtips that proud and shtately-loike, you'd think he owned the
　　town,
And houlds his shtick convenient to be tappin' some wan down—
Aich blissed day, I watch to see him comin' up the sthrate,
For by the greatest bit of luck, our house is on his bate."

Russell's crowning effort was a piece of dialect
verse entitled The First Banjo.　It appeared in
Scribner's, and is worthy of reprint here:

THE FIRST BANJO.

Go 'way fiddle !—folks is tired o' hearin' you a-squawkin'.
Keep silence fur yo' betters—don't you heah de banjo talkin' ?
About de 'possum's tail she's gwine to lecter—ladies, listen !—
About de ha'r what isn't dar, an' why de ha'r is missin'.

"Dar's gwine to be an oberflow," said Noah, lookin' solemn—
For Noah tuk the Herald, an' he read de ribber column—
An' so he sot his hands to work a-cl'arin' timber-patches,
An' 'lowed he's gwine to build a boat to beat de steamah "Natchez."

Ol' Noah kep' a-nailin', an' a-chippin', an' a-sawin' ;
An' all de wicked neighboirs kep' a-laughin' an' a-pshawin' ;
But Noah didn't min' 'em—knowin' what wuz gwine to happen ;
An' forty days and forty nights de rain it kept a-drappin'.

Now, Noah had done cotched a lot ob ebery sort o' beas'es—
Ob all de shows a-trabbelin' it beat 'em all to pieces !
He had a Morgan colt, an' sebral head o' Jarsey cattle—
An' drew 'em 'board de ark as soon's he heared de thunder rattle.

Den sech anoder fall ob rain !—it come so awful hebby
De ribber riz immegitly, an' bursted troo de lebbee ;
De people all wuz drownded out—'cept Noah an' de critters,
An' men he'd hired to work de boat—an' one to mix de bitters.

De ark she kep' a-sailin', an' a-sailin', an' a-sailin';
De lion got his dander up, an' like to bruk de palin'—
De sarpints hissed—de painters yelled—tell—what wid all de fussin',
You c'u'd'n't hardly heah de mate a-bossin' roun' an' cussin'.

Now, Ham, de only niggar what wuz runnin' on de packet,
Got lonesome in de barber-shop, and c'u'dn't stan' de racket;
An' so, for to amuse he-self, he steamed some wood an' bent it,
An' soon he had a banjo made—de fust dat wuz invented.

He wet de ledder, stretched it on; made bridge, an' screws, an' apron;
An' fitted in a proper neck—'twas bery long and tap'rin';
He tuk some tin and twisted him a thimble for to ring it ;
An' den de mighty question riz: how wuz he gwine to string it ?

De 'possum had as fine a tail as dis dat I's a singin';
De ha'r's so long, an' thick, an' strcng—jes' fit for banjo stringin'—
Dat niggar shaved 'em off as short as washday dinner graces ;
An' sorted ob 'em by de size, from little E's to basses.

He strung her, tuned her, struck a jig—'twas Nebber Min' de Wedder—
She soun' like forty-lebben bands a-playin' all togedder;
Some went to pattin', some to dancin'; Noah called de figgers—
An' Ham he sot an' knocked de tune, de happiest ob niggars !

Now, sence dat time—it's mighty strange—dere's not de slightest
    showin'.
Ob any ha'r upon de cunnin' 'possum's tail a-growin';
An' curi's too—dat nigger's ways ; his people nebber los' 'em—
For, whar you finds de niggar, dar's de banjo an' de possum !

JOHN H. WILLIAMS.

Mr. J. H. Williams, better known as "the Norristown Herald man," is one of the few successful latter-day humorists. He was born in Montgomery county, Pennsylvania, and after a few years of common school education, he located in Norristown, a lively town of the Keystone State, serving an apprenticeship as a printer's devil. In 1860 he began writing for the New York Mercury over the signature of "B. Dadd." About this time he also produced a series of letters signed "A. Ward, Jr.," which, by the way, were excellent imitations, and were widely copied, some papers dropping the Jr. and crediting them to Artemus Ward himself. For several years Williams resided in Wilmington, Delaware, but in 1871 he returned to Norristown and became attached to the Herald. Williams is considered one of the most rollicking writers on the American press. He is still a young man and has been married for several years. He forbade my writing a biography for him and begged of me to allow him to compose his own "obituary," as he is pleased to call it. Here is what he wrote:

"MY DEAR MR. CLEMENS:

"A man's biography auto always be written by himself. A disinterested party is liable to omit some of the facts. A personal history should above all things be truthful—devoid of fulsomeness, and embrace all the important events of its subject's life, good or bad. Too many biographers lie like a patent medicine advertisement. This is to be regretted.

"My memory is too treacherous to write my own life anyhow. I have been informed that I was present on the occasion of my birth, but I haven't the slightest recollection of it—as some one has previously remarked.

"I am older—am uglier—than I was two score years ago.

"Then, young ladies would chuck me under the chin and gushingly exclaim: "B'ess its purty 'ittle heart."

"Now—they don't.

"And I am rather glad of it, for the aforesaid young ladies must be nearly sixty years old now, and some of them wear glasses and decayed teeth. If I had time, dear reader, I could tell you how, in 1492, under the nom de plume of Christopher Columbus, I discovered America. This is a fact not generally known. Sometimes it seems like a wild, weird dream. You may have read something about the discovery. It was considered important at the time ; but more than one person, no doubt, upon looking around and seeing the distressing amount of misery in America, and observing how bogus mining companies, policy shops, rowing matches, political corruption and other frauds flourish like a green baize, will regret that I ever discovered it.

" I have one wife.

" I could, if my other duties permitted, describe how, in 1773, I surrounded thirty-two wild Indians, and after a hand-to-hand conflict lasting seven hours, I killed twenty-four of the redskins, wounded sixteen, and took eleven prisoners. The remainder fled. Aside from being pierced by twenty-one arrows, I escaped without a scratch.

" And yet I was never made the hero of a dime novel ! Probably because I didn't wear long hair and a soft hat as big around as a cart wheel.

" I am not addicted to bicycle riding—and therefore still retain the respect of my neighbors.

" If it was not my hour to go out and see a man, it would afford me great pleasure to allude to the day that I landed at Plymouth Rock, with a lot of pilgrims, without any "rocks" in my pocket. I shall never do it again.

" I never wrote a comic opera.

"This assertion, if made public, would be received with an air—or rather a tornado of incredulity. It would be accepted as a wild, reckless piece of exaggeration. And yet it is a positive fact.

" I shall not refer to the time I fell at Bunker Hill—caused by stepping on a banana skin,—nor mention the fact that I once struck a gentleman called Billy Patterson. I forgot the date of the latter event; but I desire to say in extenuation that Mr. Patterson struck me first. And yet he had the facial prominence to sue me for assault and battery. However, the grand jury ignored the bill, and saddled the cost upon the plaintiff.

" I have never—never, understand, without any 'hardly' qualification about it—lectured.

" My wife has, to an audience of one.

" I don't suppose it would interest the general public to know that, about sixty years ago, while at breakfast, I was blown up with dynamite, by a party of enraged subscribers of our paper. Their provocation was great, but I think they were a little too impetuous, as it were. In an unguarded moment, I printed the alleged pun, 'What did the corn-brake?' and thousands of our subscribers nearly lost their reason trying to discover the joke, which they naturally thought must lurk therein.

About fifty of them arose in their might,—and dynamite,—and elevated things. I lost two arms and two legs. But this was not the worst. A religious weekly chromo was irreparably ruined. Perhaps I should explain that the arms and legs belonged to a chair and a table, respectively.

"This little incident effectually cured me of punning in print. I have not made a joke since.

"I invented the 'fifteen puzzle,' but I would rather not have this piece of imprudence made known until I get my life heavily insured.

"Since 1850 I have killed my grandmother, burned an orphan asylum, embezzled fifty thousand dollars, and committed arson. These facts came out soon after I was nominated for a political office. They came out in an opposition paper. They always do; and the only way to prevent their appearance is to buy the paper— or its editor.

"I have never been in jail or in Congress— though there may be worse people in both pla—. But, as I remarked at the outset, I am compelled to forego the pleasure of sending you a biographical sketch. I suppose my esteemed friend, Eli Perkins, would write one for me for a mere pittance, but I would rather journey through life without a biography to my back, than to have one that does not breathe the spirit of truth, in every line—truth that is neither warped nor bent— sweet, pure, undefiled truth that will wash.

"Yours, etc.,

J. H. WILLIAMS."

JAMES M. BAILEY.

Albany, New York, claims Mr. James M. Bailey, of the Danbury News, as her offspring. The boyhood days of the Danbury News man were characterized by nothing unusual or exciting. At an early age he left school and sought a situation in a grocery store. As a grocer, James proved an utter failure, and without hesitation left his newly found occupation, and soon after took to the law, building air castles of a great and glorious future.

Not satisfied, however, with the fullness of his money coffers, Bailey deserted the law to seek a more profitable business. He gave up all professional desires and turned mechanic, serving two long years as a carpenter. But in 1862 the war of the Rebellion again changed his occupation, and Bailey, with all the patriotism of an American youth, enlisted as a private in the Seventh regiment of Connecticut volunteers. For three years he fought with a desperation only equalled by his desperate attempts at producing puns in after years.

In the early part of 1866 Bailey, in company with T. Donovan, purchased the Danbury (Connecticut) Times. In 1870 the firm purchased the only opposition paper in the town, and named the result of the combination the Danbury News. In 1873 Bailey made a trip to California, and in April of the next year went to Europe, where he remained until 1875. During these travels he wrote constantly for his paper, and by so doing acquired the title of "the Danbury News Man."

In 1873 Bailey issued, through the Boston house of Lee & Shepard, his first volume of humorous sketches, under the caption of Life in Danbury. The book had a tremendous sale for several years, and fully fifty thousand copies were sold. In the fall of the same year he produced an almanac, the first and last work of the kind he ever published.

As a lecturer Bailey has never been a great success. Perhaps if he had entered the lecture field in 1874, at which time he was far more popular than at any time during his life, he would have realized a small fortune from his lectures. But as a speaker he never made the name he has acquired through his writings. In 1877, They all Do It was issued and so well was the volume received that the Danbury News Man's name again became a household word. Another work which appeared in 1879, also became quite popular. It was entitled Mr. Phillips' Goneness.

Bailey's first humorous paragraph appeared in the News in 1872, and, by January of the next year, his productions were being published in almost every paper in the country. About this time a special edition of the News was issued for general circulation throughout the country. It took exceedingly well for several years, but was discontinued about two years ago. Bailey has acquired his fame and fortune through his own endeavors and struggles in the world. He is a self-made man in every respect. He is quite prepossessing in his personal appearance, his manner is dignified and pleasing, his demeanor modest and unassuming, and his countenance honest and frank. In his face there is nothing to note his humor, save the merry, bright, and unmistakable twinkle of the eye.

Some time ago an entertainment was given in New York, in honor of Robert J. Burdette, of the Burlington Hawkeye. To W. A. Croffut, who gave the entertainment, the Danbury News Man wrote the following letter of request:

"MY DEAR CROFFUT:— Your invitation received, and I thank you heartily for it, while I regret that I am unable to accept it. Age and the cares of life (I have two of the puzzles) are giving me away, and prevent me from taking a journey to your city. Besides we are getting ready to move, and my wife feels that much of the symmetry of the performance would be lost, if I were not here to permeate it with my presence. One of our carpets is so worn that it could hardly be trusted in the hands of a stranger, and it will be necessary for me to shake it in person. This I cannot very well avoid, or I would. Confidentially, my desire to be here is to prevent the removal to the new house of about two tons of old rubbish that no one but a woman would think of carting around. You are married and will understand me. Give my regards to the guest of the evening, and tell him that I hope to have the pleasure some time of taking him by the hand.

"Yours sincerely,

J. M. BAILEY."

CHARLES H. SMITH.

Charles H. Smith (Bill Arp) is one of the oldest of living humorists. Under the *nom de plume* of Bill Arp he has given the world some very rich things in the way of humor, and the columns of the Atlanta (Georgia) Constitution, have, during the past few years, teemed with his witty, sparkling letters. Bill Arp is known all over the South, and in many of the Gulf States his reputation is equal to that of Mark Twain.

Mr. Smith lives in a retired manner at his country-seat near Cartersville, Georgia. From this rural retreat, he writes me of his life as follows:

"Speaking as though I was another fellow, let me say that—Major Charles H. Smith was born in Lawrenceville, Georgia, June 15, 1826—that is to say, the 'major' part was not born then, though I suppose he was born all at once, but the title, the prefix, the dignity I mean, wasn't born to him until June, 1861, when he was knighted by Jeff Davis, and assigned to the staff of Colonel Barton, with aspirations more sanguine than sanguinary. The Major used to be a 'peace colonel,' but was reduced to a war major, for you must know that these peace colonels abounded in the land. There was no harm in them, and the title signified only a patriotic devotion to the political fortunes of the governor—that is, the commander in chief.

"You must know, if you do not, that Georgia boasted of an army and navy in the good old times. The navy was altogether imaginary, picturesque, esthetic, and did not muster nor parade; but the army was a fact, and was mobilized twice a year, not in corpses, or cores, or whatever you call them, but in brigades and regiments, in each county, and as the commander in chief could not be in every county at the same time to review his 'meelish,' he had to attend by proxy, therefore he appointed a proxy in every county, with the rank of colonel. This honor when conferred was intended as a kind of mucilage that cemented the donee to the donor, and the donee was expected to cry 'encore' if the donor wanted to be re-elected to the gubernatorial chair. Parties were pretty equally balanced in Georgia, and every time we had a new governor we had a new set of colonels, say an hundred or more, on the average, every two or four years. This is how we boasted of so many peace colonels, for when a man once got the title he kept it, no matter if he didn't keep the office. All this is to explain how Major Smith came to be a colonel under Governor Howell Cobb, and was afterwards reduced to his present rank. He says he really prefers the minor title to the major, for it is based on a war footing, and besides, the ladies have a way of saying 'major' with a softer and sweeter inflection than they used to say colonel.

"The Major was born and bred as usual, but his singular parentage is to be made a note of. His father was a Massachusetts man, and his mother a native of Charleston. This combination was happy enough in itself, but developed in the 'boy' a disposition to fits of passion, on which occasions he used to bite himself and bump his head against the door, but his good mother always said he couldn't help it, for it was South Carolina fighting Massachusetts.

"The Major's father was a merchant, and as the boy grew up he trained him to trade and traffic behind the counter. Later in life he sent him 'to a manual labor institute, where the boys were expected to pay for their board by working in the field three hours every day. Presumptuous expectation ! It generally took the boys about three hours to find their tools and get ready for work. Link pins were stolen, and by the time the wagon reached the field the wheel came off. When the overseer was watching one squad another slipped off to the creek to go in bathing, and so in due time the school collapsed. The 'boy' was next initiated into the mysteries of riding the mail to a neighboring village. This was not considered a very elegant or aristocratic occupation. The steed was a kind of equine dromedary, and jogged along at his leisure without regard to whip or spur. The monotony of this employment became very monotonous to the boy, and gave him abundant leisure for mental exercise.

"There is nothing romantic or thrilling about riding an old-fashioned mail—nothing like the long express across the plains that Mark Twain has so bewitchingly described in Roughing It; no fleet-footed mustang, no 'ostler standing with another ready at the station, no running against time, no passing returning post-boys with a smile and a salute, no nothing but an occasional old woman coming to the fence with a pair of socks she wanted to send to town to exchange for indigo or copperas, and as she looked over her spectacles inquired 'Are you the mail boy?' The youth sometimes looked smilingly at her as he replied: 'Why—yes—mam, you didn't think I was a female boy, did you?'

"In due time the boy graduated at this business,

and his father sent him to college. He had as good a time there as is usual. He made many pleasant acquaintances, some lasting friendships, and a love or two, and at the close of his career married a daughter of Judge Hutchins. He next studied law with the judge, and after his admission to the bar, removed to Rome, Georgia, and founded a partnership with Judge Underwood, a gentleman noted for his ability, both as a judge and a statesman. This partnership was pleasant and profitable. It was obliged to be profitable as a matter of necessity, for it continued until there were a score of children in the two families, and paternal ancestors knew but little of economy, or its prudence of laying up money for a rainy day.

" Prior to the war Major Smith had frequently indulged his inclinations for humorous and critical observations on men and measures, but it was not until the spring of 1861 that his peculiar genius found a field rich enough to harvest in. The famous proclamation of President Lincoln, ordering the people of the rebellious South to 'cease their turbulent demonstrations and to disband their military companies, and disperse and retire to their homes, within thirty days, under penalty of being arrested and tried for treason,' seemed very ludicrous and absurd to the hot bloods of the South, who really felt like they could whip all the world and the rest of mankind, and so the Major burlesqued it in his way as though he was an un-lettered countryman who wanted to disperse but couldn't. He said he 'had done his darndest to disperse, but the boys were so hot that when you throwed water on 'em they sizzed, and that was the way they was making up their companies.' If a boy 'sizzed' they took him, and if he didn't, they didn't, and he respectfully asked 'Mr. Link-horn' for a little more time.

"The Major read his manuscript to two or three friends in his office, and at the conclusion noticed that the original Bill Arp stood at the door a list-ener.   .

"Bill's merry eyes seemed to enjoy it, and he came forward with a query, 'Colonel,' said he, 'are you gwine to print that?'

"'I think I will, Bill,' said he.

"'What name are you gwine to put to it?' said Bill.

"'I don't know, Bill,' said he.

"'Well, put mine, by golly; for them's my sen-timents,' said Bill, and so Bill Arp's name was put to please him, and it was thus that the *nom de plume* was acquired. This same Bill Arp kept a ferry near Rome, and was so fond of hearing law-yers talk that he would slip off from his ferry dur-ing court week and stay all day in the court house,

or he would frequent their office just to get into
good company.   He was wholly unlettered, could
neither read nor write, but had a good mother wit
of his own, and was never considered an interloper
by any sociable crowd.   He was wont to say that
every poor man ought to be tackled on to a rich
one; that he belonged to Colonel Johnston, and
didn't want a better master.   He was asked one
day who he was going to vote for, and says he:
'I don't know, till I see Colonel Johnston, and he
won't know, till he see Judge Underwood, and the
Judge won't know till he hears from Alexander
Stephens, but who in the dickens tells Alec Stephens, I'll be dogged if·I know.'

"Bill Arp joined the army with the Major, in the
same command, on June 8, 1861.   Bill lost two
sons in the conflict, but got through safe himself,
and lived until 1878.   Peace to his ashes.

"In 1866 Major Smith was unanimously chosen
to represent his district as State Senator, and was
made chairman of the financial committee.   This
is the only official dignity he has borne, and this
was wholly unsought.   In 1877 he retired from
his profession to the more peaceful and congenial
pursuit of tilling the soil, and seems extremely
happy in his communion with nature and the quiet
seclusion of his family from the follies and cares of
society life.   He has ten living children, and has

a lot of grandchildren coming on, whose greatest
delight is to go to grandpa's and play in the branch
and catch minnows, ride the colts, and hunt hens'
nests, and fish all the day long.   The Major says
a grandparent has no business living in town, on a
half-acre lot, for it is no pleasure to the grandchildren to visit him and grandma in a pent up Utica
or a Rome either.   They want latitude and longi-
tude, so let grandparents move into the country,
where the little chaps can come and go, and spread
out and 'holler,' and be happy.   Solomon says
that children's children are the glory of a man,
and there is nothing better to work for than glory."

In a recent letter to the author of this volume
Major Smith tells a funny story in his own peculiar style.   He says:

"Speaking of children, reminds me of Dr.
Johnston, and so I must tell you that I spent a few
days last winter with General Loring, who was
born and bred a soldier.   He was in the cavalry
service in the far West with Fremont and Carson
all his youth, next in the confederate army as a
major-general, and next as chief of the Khedive's
army in Egypt.   He returned laden with glory
and honors, and fine clothes.   He had his servant
man to dress in the Khedive's jeweled suit for my
inspection.   He showed me his portfolio of splen-
did engravings, and photographs of all the notable

things in the old world. Every few pages we
would come to the photo of a beautiful woman,
and he would carelessly remark : 'Only a lady
friend of mine.' The General is a bachelor of
some sixty years, and I so much admired his conversation, I ventured to say that he ought to write
a book of his travels and exploits, and reminded
him what Dr. Johnston said to Boswell : 'Every
man owes something to posterity, a debt that he
can and ought to pay. He should do one or more
of three things. Plant a tree, the shade of which,
or the fruit of which would pleasure him, or write
a book, the sentiments of which would benefit
him, or—get a child that would be an honor to
the human race.'

"'Now, General,' said I, 'Have you ever written a book ?'

"'No,' said he.

"'Have you ever planted a tree ?'

"'Never,' said he.

"'Have you ever begotten a child ?'

"'None to speak of,' said he."

A. MINER GRISWOLD.

Alphonso Miner Griswold was born near Utica, Oneida county, New York, January 26, 1834. His youth was spent in the usual way, and in 1856 he graduated at Hamilton college, with more or less honor. It was not until November, 1857, that "Gris" entered the journalistic world by accepting a position as reporter on the Buffalo Daily Times, then owned and edited by the late Henry W. Faxen. When the Times was merged into the Republic, Griswold transferred his talents to the latter sheet.

In May, 1858, Griswold began writing under the *nom de plume* of "The Fat Contributor." His humor was racy and original, and he was classed among the leading fun makers of the day. He went to Detroit in the autumn of 1858, and accepted a position on the Advertiser. A year later he removed his talents to Cleveland, where he labored in the office of the Plain Dealer, published by Hon. W. W. Armstrong. He succeeded Artemus Ward as assistant editor, and during the early part of the war he wrote many patriotic and ringing editorials. After a brief season on the Cleveland Leader, "Gris" removed to Cincinnati, and in 1863 became a member of the staff of the Evening Times, which position he continued to hold for nearly ten years.

In the latter part of 1872, in company with others, he began the publication of the Cincinnati Saturday Night, a journal which now enjoys a prosperous existence. He became the sole proprietor of the paper in 1874, and was for some years assisted in his labors by his wife, a lady of numerous scholarly attainments.

Griswold resides in a quiet, out-of-the-way street, just off the busy thoroughfares of the Queen City of the West, and lives in a retired, happy manner. During later years he has occasionally made a lecture tour, delivering his famous lecture, Injun Meal, and others to delighted audiences.

· Artemus Ward and Griswold were the best of friends, and the "Fat Contributor" tells many anecdotes of his experience in the world alongside of Browne. Speaking of Artemus' Ward, in a humorous way, Griswold once said in a humorous article:

"When, in 1863, Ward conceived the idea of making a lecture tour through California—a great undertaking in those days—he offered me, to accompany him as agent, a salary that would cause the insignificant pay of a Cleveland local to blush with shame. Not knowing that lecturers, and especially humorists, have a way of engaging every man as agent who professes a desire to travel, I made all preparations to go, resigned my situation, and anxiously awaited my summons.

As I waited, various articles were sold to pay expenses. I ate my stove I remember, and I think I drank up my bureau. At length, when nearly everything had gone, I believe that Ward had gone, too, taking another agent. I was naturally incensed, and resolved that there would be a severe settlement when next we met. I rehearsed the anticipated scene frequently, and resolved how I would go to work and annihilate him.

"Our meeting was in New York in July, 1864. I had heard of his return from California, and prepared to empty the vials of wrath upon his head. We accidentally ran against each other on Broadway. My slumbering indignation flamed up at once. I thought of the cooking stove I had devoured, and the various articles of household furniture I drank up, and was about to go for him when Ward suddenly rushed forward, and, grasping me warmly by the hand, exclaimed:

" 'Why, Gris., old boy, how are you? *When did you get back from California?* '

"As I looked at him, speechless with amazement, he continued: 'They told me you came home around the "horn," but I never knew you to go around a horn yet—join me!'

"Now Ward had a very persuasive way of locking his arm in with another's, and in a momentary fit of weakness, I went along.

"'Ward!' said I sternly, 'I owe you a licking on account of the California agency business, but will put it off until we drink.'

"'Put it off as long as you want to,' replied Ward, in a tone of generous accommodation, as though I was speaking about returning him a loan. 'If you owe me a licking, pay me when you get ready. I am in no hurry. Don't care if you never pay it.'

"Numerous were the unavailing efforts that I made to bring Ward to a settlement. When I would commence: 'Now, Artemus, how about that California business?' he would interrupt— 'Oh, never mind that whipping. No hurry at all. Send it to me through the mail—or telegraph it. Let's drink.'

"I have got even with Browne, however, in a measure—I have *engaged* a number of agents myself."

BILL NYE.

Away out in the wilds of Wyoming Territory, in the fast growing city of Laramie, dwells one of the most noted funny men of to-day. Bill Nye is a modest looking name, and at first sight looks like a *nom de plume;* yet Bill Nye is the "only and original" of that name. He is a young man, and has been in the journalistic profession only three or four years. He began work on the Laramie City Boomerang, and is at present the managing editor of that publication. The Boomerang is a newspaper of metropolitan proportions, and issues both daily and weekly editions.

Bill Nye has, during the past two years, written a larger quantity and a better quality of first-class, genuine humor, than any other funny man in America. He is widely quoted, and has issued one book entitled, Bill Nye and his Mule Boomerang. This volume was issued in Chicago in 1881, and had a tremendous sale. Like others of his class, Nye is modest, and prefers to relate to the awaiting world his own misfortunes, in his own peculiar style.   He writes as follows:

"MY DEAR CLEMENS: I herein make a few brief statements, which you are at liberty to enlarge upon in such a way as to give my life that odor of holy calm and unblemished smirchlessness which will sound well in history.

"I was born on the 25th day of August, A. D., 1850, somewhere in the State of Maine.   I do not remember where.   It was either along the Atlantic seaboard, or on the Kennebec river, and the exact spot has escaped my memory.   As soon as I could walk I left Maine and came west, where I have been for about thirty years.

"Looking over my whole eventful career, I see nothing to regret, except the fact that I was born in Maine.   Probably the State of Maine regrets it as much as I do."

"My early childhood was spent in acquiring knowledge relative to the habits and movements of the bumble-bee and the water-melon.

"There is nothing in particular, perhaps, to distinguish my youth from that of other eminent men.   I did not study the Greek grammar by the light of a pine knot when I was a child.   I did not think about it.   Had I supposed that I would ever rise to the proud pinnacle of fame, I might have filled my system full of deceased languages, but as it was, I thought I was in luck to acquire sufficient education. to last me from one meal to another.

" I did not do any smart things as a child. It remained for later years to bring out the latent genius and digestive strength which I now possess. I did not graduate first in my class. I did not rise to distinction in two weeks. I did not dazzle the civilized world with my sterling ability. I just plugged along from day to day, and when I had an afternoon to myself it did not occur to me that I might read Horace, or Cicero, or the dictionary. I fooled away those priceless moments carrying water to the elephant, so that I could acquire information at the circus.

"My journalistic career has been short, but full of interest. Though only covering a' space of three 'or four years, it has been rich in amusement and gory personal encounter.

" The West is well known as the home of fearless and deadly journalism. It brings out all there is in a man and throws him upon his own resources. It also throws him down stairs if he is not constantly on his guard.

" I a man attorney by profession and a newspaper man by force of circumstances. I am married and have been for five years. I do not regret this step.

"I am six feet high, of commanding appearance, and would be selected in any audience as a man who would not rob an overland train while there was anyone looking.

"I am in robust health, with the exception of a corn, which I inherited from the old stock of Nyes, who first invaded the free lunch counters of of Skouhegan, Maine.

"To any one who is curious to investigate my career while in the West, I would say that I cheerfully refer them to any vigilance committee of this section.

"If I can throw any more light on this delicate topic, or should the public care for a fuller diagnosis, I am always at your service.

· BILL NYE.

"LARAMIE CITY, Wyoming, January 27, 1882."

There is no doubt that during later years Bill Nye has been more extensively copied than any other humorist of the day.   Among the hundreds of good things he has produced, I select a few of the most touching and pathetic:

THE ENGLISH JOKE.

The average English joke has its peculiarities. A sort of mellow distance, a kind of chastened reluctance, a coy and timid, yet trusting, though evanescént intangibility which softly lingers in the troubled air, and lulls the tired senses to dreamy rest, like the subdued murmur of a hoarse jackass about nine miles up the gulch. He must be a hardened wretch indeed, who has not felt his bosom heave and the scalding tears steal down his furrowed cheek after he has read an English joke. There can be no hope for the man who has not been touched by the gentle, pleading, yet all potent, sadness embodied in the humorous paragraph of the true Englishman. One may fritter away his existence in chasing follies of our day and generation, and have naught to look back upon but a choice assortment of robust regrets, but if he will stop in his mad career to read an English pun, his attention will be called to the solemn thought that life is, after all, but a tearful journey to the tomb. Death and disaster on every hand may fail to turn the minds of a thoughtless world to serious matters, but when the London funny man grapples with a particularly skittish and evasive joke, with its weeping willow attachment, and hurls it at a giddy and reckless humanity, a prolonged wail of anguish goes up from broken hearts and a sombre pall hangs in the gladsome sky like a pair of soldier pants with only one suspender.

MR. NYE EMBARRASSED.

There was an entertainment at Laramie a few evenings ago, at which the guests appeared in such costumes as their taste suggested. The following will give some idea of the occasion:

Mr. Nye wore a Prince Albert coat with tails caught back with red jeans, and home made sunflowers. He also wore a pair of velvet knee breeches, which, during the evening, in an unguarded moment, split up the side about nine feet. This, together with the fact that one of his long black stockings got caught on the top of a window cornice, tearing a small hole in it, letting out the saw-dust and baled hay with which he was made up, seemed to cast a gloom over the countenance of this particular guest. With one large voluptuous calf, and the other considerably attenuated, Mr. Nye seemed more or less embarrassed.

JOSEPH C. NEAL.

A series of humorous descriptive articles, known as Charcoal Sketches, appeared in 1837 in a Philadelphia newspaper. They became famous, and for years their author was noted as a leading American humorist. Joseph C. Neal, the author of the Charcoal Sketches, was born on the third day of February, 1807, in the town of Greenland, New Hampshire. His father had for many years been the principal of a popular academy in Philadelphia, but his health failing him, he was compelled to retire to a country residence at Greenland, where, along with his other duties, he officiated as pastor in the Congregational church of the village.

When the subject of this sketch was two years old his father died, and the family soon after removed to Philadelphia, and thence to Pottsville, in the same State. Mr. Neal resided here until 1831, when he settled in Philadelphia, and assumed the duties of editor of the Pennsylvanian, a journal which became very popular, and conspicuous for its influence on the political character of the State.

It was in the office of this journal that the elder James Gordon Bennett passed a portion of his early years in journalism.

For nearly ten years Mr. Neal devoted his talents to the Pennsylvanian, but at length his health failed him, and in 1841 he went abroad, traveling in Europe and Africa for nearly two years. In 1844 he retired from the editorial chair of the Pennsylvanian, and established in the autumn of the same year a weekly literary miscellany, under the title of Neal's Saturday Gazette. Neal's reputation as a writer secured for the Gazette an immediate and continued success.

Joseph C. Neal's humorous sketches of that character for which he afterwards became distinguished, first appeared in the Pennsylvanian under the title of "City Worthies." These sketches were reprinted and praised in hundreds of American newspapers. In 1837 he published Charcoal Sketches, or Scenes in a Metropolis. In these sketches he drew from life a class of characters peculiar to the lower classes and disreputable haunts in large cities. The appearance of the sketches in book form was hailed with delight, and several large editions were readily disposed of. The work was also republished in London under the auspices of Charles Dickens, who took a great interest in the American humorist and his works.

In 1844 Mr. Neal issued his second book, Peter Ploddy and Other Oddities, and soon after, another and newer series of Charcoal Sketches. Both of these books commanded a large and ready sale. Neal continued to edit the Saturday Gazette until July 3, 1848, when he died very suddenly at his home in Philadelphia, of a complication of diseases. His widow published a second and revised edition of his works some years after his death.

Soon after his death, R. W. Griswold, in his Prose Writers of America, said of Mr. Neal: "He writes as if he had little or no sympathy with his creations, and as if he were a calm spectator of acts and actors, whimsical or comical,—an observer rather by accident than from desire. . . . . His style is compact and pointed, abounding in droll combinations and peculiar phrases, which have the ease and naturalness of transcripts of real conversations. He had too much good nature to be caustic, and too much refinement to be coarse. In some of his sketches he exhibits not only a happy faculty for the burlesque, and singular skill in depicting character, but a generality and heartiness of appreciation which carry the reader's feelings along with his fancy."

The following selection from Peter Ploddy will tend to show Mr. Neal's peculiar style of writing:

"'Common people, Billy—low, common people, can't make it out when nature raised a gentleman in the family—a gentleman all complete, only the money's been forgot. If a man won't work all the time—day in and day out—if he smokes by the fire, or whistles out of the winder, the very gals bump agin him, and say, "Git out of the way, loaf!"

"'But, Billy, my son, never mind, and keep not a lettin' on," continued Nollikens, and a beam of hope irradiated his otherwise Saturnine countenance; "the world's a railroad, and the cars is comin' —all we'll have to do is to jump in, chalked free. There will be a time—something must happen. Rich widders are about yet, though they are snapped up so fast. Rich widders, Billy, are "special providences," as my old boss used to say when I broke my nose in the entry, sent here like rafts to pick up deservin' chaps when they can't swim no longer. When you've bin down twy'st, Billy, and are jist off agin, then comes the widder afloatin' along. Why, splatter docks is nothin' to it, and a widder is the best of all life-preservers, when a man is most a case, like you and me.'

"'Wall, I'm not perticklar, not I, nor never was. I'll take a widder, for my part, if she's got the mint drops, and never ask no questions. I'm not proud—never was harrystocratic—I drinks with anybody, and smokes all the cigars they give me. What's the use of bein' stuck up, stiffy? It's my principle that other folks are nearly as good as me, if they're not constables nor aldermen. I can't stand them sort.'

" 'No, Billy,' said Nollikens, with an encouraging smile, 'no, Billy, such indiwidooals as them don't know human natur'—but, as I was agoin to say, if there happens to be a short crop of widders, why can't somebody leave us a fortin?—that will do as well if not better. Now look here— what's easier than this? I'm standin' on the wharf—the rich man tries to go aboard of the steamboat—the niggers push him off the plank— in I jumps, ca-splash! The old gentleman isn't drowned ;' but he might have been drowned but for me, and if he had a bin, where's the use of his money then? So he gives me as much as I want now, and a great deal more when he defuncts riggler, accordin' to law and the practice of civilized nations. You see—that's the way the thing works. I'm at the wharf every day—can't afford to lose a chance, and I begin to wish the old chap would hurry about comin' along. What can keep him?'

" 'If it 'ud come to the same thing in the end,' remarked Billy Bunkers, 'I'd rather the niggers would push the old man's little boy into the water,

if it's all the same to him.   Them fat old fellers
are so heavy when they're skeered, and hang on
so—why I might get drowned before I had time
to go to the bank with the check!   But what's the
use of waitin'?   Couldn't we shove 'em in some
warm afternoon ourselves?   Who'd know in the
crowd?'

" ' I've thought of that, Bunkers, when a man
was before me who looked the right sort,—but,
Billy, there might be mistakes—perhaps, when you
got him out, he couldn't pay.   What then?'

" ' Why, keep puttin new ones to soak every day,
till you fish up the right one.'

" ' It won't do,—my friend—they'd smoke the
joke—all the riffraff in town would be pushin' old
gentlemen into the river, and the elderly folks
would have to give up travelin' by the steamboat.
We must wait till the real thing happens.   The
right person will be sure to come along.'

" ' I hope so ; and so it happens quick, I don't
much care whether the old man, his little boy, or
the rich widder gets the ducking.   I'm not proud.'

" ' Then you'll see me come the nonsense over
the old folks—who's loafer now?—and my dog
will bite their cat—who's ginger pop, and jam
spruce beer, at this present writin', I'd like to
know?'

"Thus, wrapped in present dreams and future an-

ticipations—a king that is to be—lives Nicholas
Nollikens—the grand exemplar of the corner
loungers. Nicholas and his tribe exist but for to-
morrow, and rely firmly on that poetic justice,
which should reward those who wait patiently until the wheel of fortune turns up a prize."

GEORGE H. DERBY.

"Before 'John Phoenix' there was scarcely any American humorist—not of the distinctly literary sort—with whom one could smile and keep one's self respect," says William Dean Howells, the novelist, in a recent magazine article. This may indeed be true, but there were others in the time of George H. Derby, better known by his *nom de plume* of John Phoenix, who were of the same school of humorists, yet they were far inferior as wits. Derby, had he lived, would have become perhaps one of the leading humorists of the country. As it was, he was known to the public as a humorous writer for only a few years before his death.

George H. Derby was born of poor but well educated parents in Norfolk county, Massachusetts, in 1823. Little is known of his boyhood or early life. He entered the West Point military academy while yet a youth, and graduated from that institution in 1846. The same year he became engaged in the war with Mexico and continued in the field during the larger part of the year following. He was present at the battle of

Vera Cruz and Cerro Gordo, and was made brevet first lieutenant at the former place. He received a severe wound during the latter engagement. He remained with the regular army at the close of the war, and was sent upon various surveys and expeditions from 1847 to 1852. During the two years following the last named date, Derby was engaged on the improvement of San Diego, California, harbor, and the next year he was on the staff of the commanding general and had charge of the military roads, department of the Pacific. In 1856 he was on the coast survey, and in the two years following was light-house engineer.

While sojourning on the Pacific coast Derby first began writing for the San Francisco papers and magazines. His contributions consisted mainly of humorous sketches written under the signature of John Phoenix. These sketches attracted general attention among the Pacific States, and in 1855 were published in book form under the title of Phoenixiana, or Sketches and Burlesques. The book was well received, and ten or twelve editions were exhausted. Four years later a second volume was issued under the title of Squibob Papers. This volume also met with a large and ready sale. Early in 1861 Derby took up his residence in New York, and produced a number of humorous sketches which were never published in book form.

He died suddenly on the 15th of May, 1861, at the age of thirty-eight. Although young in years and not having reached the acme of his fame, his work still lives and is recognized as one of the most prominent species of American humor.

Derby's humor is something like that of Artemus Ward, yet it is peculiarly original and is vastly different from the writings of the so-called funny men of the present day. Among the many good things from Derby's pen are the following:

LATE.

Passing by one of our doggeries about 3 A. M. the other morning, from which proceeded "a sound of revelry by night," a hapless stranger on his homeward way paused to obtain a slight refreshment, and to the host he said: "It appears to me your visitors are rather late to-night." "Oh, no," replied the worthy landlord, "the boys of San Diego generally run for forty-eight hours, stranger; *it's a little late for night before last*, but for to-night! why, it's just in the shank of the evening." Volumes could not have said more.

FOR SALE.

A valuable law library, lately the property of a distinguished legal gentleman of San Francisco, who who has given up practice and removed to the Farralone Islands. It consists of one volume of

"Hoyle's Games," complete and may be seen at
this office

Back numbers of the Democratic Review,
speeches and writings of Jefferson, Coffroth, Cal-
houn, Bigler, Van Buren and others.   Copies of
the San Joaquin Republican, files of the Times
and Transcript (a few at a time), and a diagram
representing the construction of the old United
States bank, for the use of a young man desirous
of turning Democrat.   Apply at this office (by
firing a gun, or punching on the ceiling, he being
deeply engaged in study in the garret), to

J. Phoenix.

AN EPITAPH.

This is all, but I writ at the time a epitaff which
I think is short, and would do to go over his grave:

> Here lies the body of James Hambrick
> Who was accidentally shot
> On the banks of the Peacus river
> By a young man.

He was accidentally shot with one of the large sized
Colt's revolvers with no stopper for the cock to rest
on it was one of the old fashion kind brass mounted
and of such is the kingdom of Heaven.

GEORGE W. PECK.

A common-sized-mustache-and-goatee young man is George W. Peck, of Milwaukee, Wisconsin. He is rather a handsome chap, and just after he has left the barber's chair he looks for all the world like a military officer. However, he looks like a common citizen when Saturday night comes around, and he has not been shaved for several days. Peck has attained quite a reputation as a humorist, through the columns of his paper, Peck's Sun. Though only established, as a weekly journal with a humorous foundation, something over two years, the Sun has already a circulation of twenty thousand copies, and is rapidly increasing.

George W. Peck is a ready writer, and takes more to the narrative style than paragraphing. His paper is well liked among his fellow humorists, and is widely quoted. Peck is still a comparatively young man, and is "fair, fat, and *thirty.*" He is one of the few newspaper men who are bashful by nature, as the following letter plainly shows:

"I do not believe the time has arrived when the American people are consumed with a desire to know where I was born, how old I am, or any of the particulars of an uneventful life. If I should ever become of so much importance, which is hardly liable to be the case, while you and I live, I will resurrect the necessary data from the orphan asylum, the reform farm, the State prison, and other places of that kind, too numerous to mention. At the present time I think it is a charity to spare the people. Whatever you do, please do not call me funny. If you do, it is very evident that you do not know me.

"Yours truly,

GEORGE W. PECK."

Here is one of Mr. Peck's recent paragraphs: "Those who take the Sun take it for the fun there is in it, and we feel a confounded sight funnier if we are making something than if we are losing. We are too old to work for glory, and too lazy to work for fun."

In a recent article in the Sun, Mr. Peck discourses as follows on the

PECULIARITIES OF THEATRICAL SUPES.

About the most laughable thing around a theatre is the "supes." However funny a play may be, the actions of the supes are funnier than the comedians. Men may act as supes for twenty years, and they can never come on the stage without appearing awkward and falling all over themselves. The actors tell them where to stand, and they get into another place. They act as if they expected to be stabbed and they cannot appear natural to save them. Take a far western scene, where they want a lot of miners in a bar-room to take a drink. One would think fellows who are in bar-rooms a dozen times a day would know how to act, but they don't. They all go up to the bar in a crowd, and fall around, and then take tin cups of alleged whiskey and stare at vacancy until told to sit down, and then they all try to sit down on the same chair. When they are wanted for a scene in the Roman forum, they get on the red night-gowns and walk around toeing in, and walking knock-kneed, making the sickest lot of Roman citizens that ever robbed a hen roost. It is a singular coincidence that a supe always has a black patch on the seat of a pair of gray pants. Where in the world they all get gray pants, and why they don't have gray patches on them, is more than anybody can find out. Let a couple of supes come on the stage to remove a table, and they will have those patches dead sure, and they will arrange to stand with the patches to the audience. They probably reason that their faces are liable to betray emotion, or that they may blush, but that the patches can maintain a stern and dignified demeanor under the most trying circumstances of guying and cat-calls on the part of the gallery boys. Female supes are even worse than men in stubbing their toes on the carpet, or backing against the wings. They are hired to come on to fill up a scene at half a dollar a night, and they usually wear octagon shaped tights, with more bran than legs, and it is painful to see them stand around. But they get confidence in themselves quicker than men, and they want to star after appearing one or two times. The supe business has lots of fun in it.

ALEXANDER EDWIN SWEET.

Texas is known to be the largest State in the Union, yet in all the vast territory there resides but one genuine humorist. Alexander Edwin Sweet is the proud possessor of that title. During the last few years the Texas Siftings has been universally quoted and ranked "A 1" among the funny papers of this country. It is needless to state in this connection that Alexander E. Sweet is one of the editors of Siftings.

Mr. Sweet is a Canadian by birth, an American by adoption, and a paragrapher and funny man by instinct. He was born in St. Johns, New Brunswick, March 28, 1841. His father was James R. Sweet, a well-known and prosperous merchant of that city. As early as 1849 young Sweet removed with his parents to San Antonio, Texas. His education was obtained at College Hill, Poughkeepsie, New York, in 1857 and 1858. The next year he went to Europe and entered the Polytechnic institute at Carlsruhe, Baden, Germany. Here he studied for several years, and in 1861 he fell in love with a handsome German girl, and led Miss Marie Zittel to the altar.

Returning to America and to Texas in 1862, he served two years in the war as a private in company A, Thirty-third regiment of Texas cavalry, Confederate army, principally on the Rio Grande, and in the Indian nation. At the close of the war he studied law in the office of Thomas I. Devine. From the law Mr. Sweet drifted into journalism, and in 1869 became editor of the San Antonio Express. In 1871, he was appointed city attorney of San Antonio by Governor Davis. Mr. Sweet had as yet written nothing of note, but with the Herald his work became widely known. Some years ago the Herald sprang into sudden fame on account of the funny articles that appeared in it, descriptive of the ludicrous side of life in Texas. The articles were copied far and wide, and then they suddenly ceased.

Mr. Sweet transferred his labors to the Galveston News and consequently that journal sprang into popularity all over the country. He possesses that peculiar journalistic trait of carrying an entire newspaper at the end of his pen. His column of Siftings in the News were widely copied, and a New York journal in commenting upon them had this to say of the author: "Mr. Sweet's sketches, paragraphs and *bon mots* are second to no living writer in freshness, originality, sparkling wit, and refined humor.   Mr. Sweet is far more than a humorous writer, as his brilliant editorials in the News from time to time will show."

A year or two ago, Mr. Sweet sought a partner in the person of Mr. J. Amroy Knox, and began the publication of Texas Siftings. Mr. Knox is also well known as an author, having written for several prominent newspapers and magazines. In conjunction with Mr. Knox, Alexander E. Sweet wrote an interesting volume, which was but recently issued from the press. It is entitled Through Texas, or from the Gulf to the Rio Grande on the back of a Mexican Mustang. The book is a narrative, descriptive and humorous, and has commanded a ready sale.

Since the establishment of Texas Siftings that journal has risen rapidly into public favor, and is sold and read in every State in the union. Mr. Sweet does the larger portion of the humorous writing for the paper. The Graphic of New York published a portrait of the rollicking humorist in 1877, but time and a heavy beard have changed him so that the picture does not now resemble him. He has a pleasant home, and surrounded by his wife and five bright children, his life is a most happy one.

Many clever articles have appeared in Texas. Siftings, but none more clever than the following:

DOMESTIC LIFE IN TEXAS.

"It wasn't that!" exclaimed Mr. Sanders, indignantly "You see, I didn't say a word at all."

"How'd she find out, then?" asked one of the party.

"Why, I went home, and she asked if it was me. I told her it was. Took the chances on that, you know. Then she asked me if I'd been drinking. I told her no. And there I stopped. Never said another word."

"But you say she caught on somewhere. How was it?"

"Just a blunder I made. When I told her I hadn't drank anything she was satisfied, but when I come to go to bed, I put on my overcoat instead of my night-shirt. That excited suspicion."

DISGUSTING GREED.

Fitznoodle is an Austin nimrod who goes out every Sunday and brings in a jack-rabbit or so. Fitznoodle is an enormous eater, and nobody else gets much of a taste of the rabbit.

"I wonder why nobody gets any of the shot except me," said Fitznoodle, taking a shot out of his mouth.

Because nobody else gets any of the rabbit, I suppose," responded Mrs. Fitznoodle, with telling sarcasm.

SAMUEL W. SMALL.

The humorous writings in the Atlanta (Georgia) Constitution have made that paper famous. It has been quoted, perhaps, as much as as any other daily newspaper in this country. Among those bright journalists employed upon its editorial staff, none have added more to the popularity of the Constitution than Samuel W. Small, better known to his admirers as "Old Si."

Small was born in Knoxville, Tennessee, in 1851, and spent his youth in that city and vicinity. In 1861 he removed to Georgia with his parents. Here he divided his time in going to school and loafing around the depots and railroad tracks. In 1865 he lived in New Orleans, and four years later he graduated from the high school in that city. After his graduation, Samuel was sent by his parents to Henry college, in Virginia, and he graduated from that institution in 1871. He then returned to Nashville, began the study of law, and was admitted to the bar by the supreme court of Tennessee in 1872.

Mr. Small failed to adopt the law as his profession and turned his entire attention to journalism. He first became a reporter on the Nashville Republican Banner, but soon after removed to Greenville, Tennessee where he edited a weekly paper, and acted as private secretary to ex-President Johnson for nearly two years. The year 1874 found him in Houston, Texas, still in the newspaper business. After laboring on nearly all the journals of Houston, he returned to Georgia in May, 1875. It was in this month that he became connected with the Atlanta Constitution, in whose columns his humorous writings first came under public notice.

The humor of Old Si, his *nom de plume*, began by his writing short and spicy paragraphs as coming from an aged negro. These grew into larger paragraphs, and gradually into lengthy articles, which were widely copied. Mr. Small is an expert stenographer and reports the official proceedings of the circuit court of Atlanta. He was connected with the Constitution, and was one of that journal's most valued writers, up to March, 1882, when he became sole editor and proprietor of a prosperous weekly paper in Florida.

In his Florida venture, the Jacksonville Union, Old Si appears as brilliant as ever, as the annexed selection will show:

FLORIDA POLITICIANS AND ALLIGATORS.

"I kinder likes dis sort ob climack!" said Old Si, as he come into the office last evening.

"In what way?"

"Well, I likes to be 'round whar yer kin hang up yer obercoat soon ez yer buys it an' set 'round in yur shurt-sleebes jest ez well on New Year ez yer kin on de Foth o' July!"

"That is pleasant."

"Yes, sah, an' dat's what meks me say what I do. Dar's plenty ob helth down heah if you jess knows how to fin' it. De only place whar you kant fin' it is in er allygator's mouf!"

"Then your advice is that people should come to Florida, but beware of the alligator?"

"Dat's hit! I ain't got no use for 'er allygator hits to much like er pollytishun—got mo' mouf dan vittals an' mo' hide dan honisty!"

And with this epigram the old man bowed himself out of the sanctum.

CHARLES HOYT.

Frederick Hudson, in his History of Journalism in America, credits the Boston Post with having originated the column of funny paragraphs which are now seen in nearly all the leading newspapers of the United States. The All Sorts column of the Post was started when that paper first appeared, over half a century ago. It was in this department that Mrs. Partington and her son Ike were first introduced to the humor-loving public, and scores of writers have sent forth their wit, during the fifty years past, through this same medium.

George F. Babbit began writing the All Sorts for the Post seven or eight years ago, but relinquished the position a few years later. Babbitt was a graduate of Harvard college, and his witticisms in the Post were of a very brilliant character. The present "funny man" of the Post is Charles Hoyt, better known to his Boston friends as Charley Hoyt.

A well-known Boston journalist in a recent article says of him: "He is a well-proportioned man, lithe, active, and nervy in physique, a broad forehead, an open face on which candor is written in every feature, bright, restless eyes, firm mouth and chin, a clear, ruddy complexion, and a voice not loud or strident but clear as a bell in its enunciation. His column of All Sorts in the Post is a fine example of conscientious paragraphing, where neither time nor diverse labor interfere to distract or hurry the writer. It is enjoyed by thousands every day, who laugh at his quaint conceits and genuine wit."

Hoyt is a native of Vermont, and comes of good, old Puritan stock. In early youth he held a public office, being page in the State Senate. In this school his intellect was sharpened, and his naturally retentive memory gathered together and carried away much which has been useful in later years. His knowledge of, and acquaintance with, public men, is wide and varied. In his personal address he is both pleasing and attractive. These are both admirable points in his favor, considering that he is a bachelor, and young at that.

Hoyt's Ragbag stories are very entertaining:

RAGBAG'S PRACTICAL JOKE.

The other night, after Mr. Ragbag had gone to bed, the idea of a very funny joke occurred to him. It seemed so funny that he went into a paroxysm of laughter, and twisted and squirmed

so that he pulled the bed clothes all out at the
foot and had to get out to tuck them in again, and
got awful cold, and made as much noise as to
awaken his wife in the next room, and she, on
hearing the cause of the commotion, told Ragbag
he was a fool and advised him to go to bed.   He
did so, but lay awake half the night thinking of
the joke, and the next morning Ragbag hastily
swallowed his breakfast, and hastened out on the
street to play his joke.   The first man he met was
Gallagher.   Gallagher's business compels him to
carry about one hundred keys, and Ragbag knew
this.   Gallagher was just the man Ragbag wanted
to see.   Rushing up to Gallagher he said:

"Ah, Gallagher, have you lost a key?"

"Don't know," replied the victim.   "Let me
see it."

"First see if you have lost one," said Ragbag.

So Gallagher took off his gloves and went to
work.   He searched pocket after pocket, and examined each and every bunch of keys carefully.
It was sharp weather, and his fingers got cold and
numb,   But he kept at it.   One hundred keys
were a good many to keep track of, and Gallagher
had to think of every lock about his establishment, and then look for that particular key, and
it was a tedious job.   And it wasn't satisfactory,
either, for Gallagher couldn't quite make up his

mind that one key was not missing. He demanded a sight of the key found. Then Ragbag's self-control gave way. With a howl of laughter he cried :

"Why, I haven't found any. I only asked if you had lost one as a matter of curiosity."

It didn't take three seconds for Gallagher to decide what to do. The snow for forty feet around was clawed and kicked into a cloud that filled the air. Folks looked out of the windows and howled to see the fun. And when Ragbag re-entered the house with his clothes torn, ear chawed, and eyes blacked, and explained that he had been playing his joke, his wife' was more than ever convinced that he was an old donkey, and told him so. Somehow, at times, humor is fearfully discouraging in this country.

HENRY CLAY LUKENS.

The New York Daily News, like all other first-class journals, possesses its paragrapher. In the person of Henry Clay Lukens, the News has for many years had a valuable contributor, and one of the best humorous writers in America. Under the name of Erratic Enrique, he has written early and late, noon, morning, and night, and, in fact, about all the time.

Lukens is of Dutch ancestry. He was born in Germantown, near Philadelphia, on the 18th day of August, 1838. His first newpaper enterprise was a monthly publication issued in his native city, during the winter of 1857. For this paper, George Alfred Townsend wrote some of his first articles. Lukens worked at his journalistic profession for many years in different States in the Union.

In 1874 he went to South America, where he remained as a traveling correspondent for nearly two years. While there he wrote interesting letters to the Danbury News and the St. John (New Brunswick) Torch, under the quaint pseudonym of Erratic Enrique. He also wrote for various other American journals under the same name.

It was not until March, 1877, that Henry Clay Lukens settled down to steady work on a daily newspaper. He then associated himself with the sprightly little News, with which paper he has ever since been connected. He originated a column of humor called Pith and Point, which has brought both the paper and himself into prominence. It is said he has not missed a week's labor since his first day's connection with the News. He is one of the few hard-worked city journalists.

Early in 1881, he began a series of articles, entitled Sanctum Sketches, in Hubbard's Advertiser, of New Haven, Connecticut. In this series of articles he produced the biographies of six or eight well known paragraphers. He is also a regular contributor to several weekly and monthly periodicals.

Lukens is quite inclined to poetry, and at times jingles some very clever and witty rhymes. The following is from his pen:

ESPRIT MALIN.

What hideous yell assails my ear?
Whose shuffling feet distract my nerves?
Insatiate demon, nothing serves
To clinch thy clutch! All day I hear,
　　　"More copy!"

My brain's a-whirl, my senses swim—
   What cares the screeching imp for that?
   He's got two words, so tonguey pat,
He slits the air with vocal vim,
                "More copy!"

A sapient smirk illumes his phiz—
   He feels his power, and grinning grips,
   The ink-wet pages, scissored slips,
And cabled specials; that's his ''biz''—
                "More copy!"

Intense disgust has hobbled hate,
   Else would I slay this vampire scorned.
   Though neither cloven-toed nor horned,
His devilish yawpings ne'er abate—
                " More copy!"

ERRATICS.

It is not so very painful to lose a fortune as it is to hear what your neighbors will say about it afterwards.

When the prodigal son comes home they no longer kill the fatted calf for him. They just turn the animal into a vaccine farm and give him the profits.

A new serial yarn by Besant and Rice is entitled, All Sorts and Conditions of Men. The plot is probably worked out in the caucus room of a delegates convention.

"Man Reading," a picture by Meissonier, has been sold for $10,000. It was cheap as dirt. The man readtng was an editor with a contribution

written on both sides of the paper, and sponta-
neously interlined besides.

Our agricultural contemporary, the Herald, has
a learned and highly interesting article on "Our
Codfish Culture." We trust it may be followed
by another, equally able, on "Our Goat Fisher-
ies." Both are subjects of intense and universal
concern.

WILLIAM A. WILKINS.

A country newspaper rarely makes its mark in the journalistic world, and especially a paper printed in such an obscure village as is Whitehall, New York. The Whitehall Times, however, is one of the few exceptions, and, although a country newspaper, has been quoted in every paper of any note in the land.

William Albert Wilkins, the editor and proprietor of the Times, and the one man who has made that journal famous, was born on the 26th day of March, 1840, in the village of Cherry Valley, Otsego county, New York. At the age of ten he removed with his parents to Cohoes, in the same State, where he attended a common district school for several years. He entered business as office boy in the village post-office. From this position he was elevated to a travelling salesman, doing business for a firm in Albany. A year later, however, he settled down to real life as a retail clothing merchant at Whitehall. In this pursuit Wilkins was quite successful, and for eleven years he continued in the business.

Wilkins says that the first important discovery of his life was when he embarked in the printing business. "Then," says he, "it was easier to convince nine-tenths of the human family that the inhabitants of the infernal regions employ their time skating on real ice ponds, than it is to convince them that they cannot conduct a live newspaper. While a merchant in the town of Whitehall, Mr. Wilkins began writing—along in the fall of 1869—several humorous communications for the Weekly Times, the very paper which he afterwards owned. His articles were signed "Hiram Green, esquire, Lait justiss of the Peece." His sketches were bright and original, and after doing all he could to supply the crusty Whitehallites with humor, he began a series of letters in the Troy Budget, which he continued for several years.

In 1870 what appeared as his guiding star shone over his horizon. A new comic weekly paper had just been introduced to the residents of New York. It was known as Punchinello, and its publisher made William Albert Wilkins, of Whitehall, a handsome offer to assume the editorial chair. Wilkins was not long in making a decision whether to accept the offer or no. In an evil moment he bade good-bye to the clothing business and hied himself to New York. His salary and the paper ended their existence in five months' time, and the Whitehall merchant was cast adrift in the great metropolis. He remained in New York and was employed with a leading wholesale clothing house until April, 1873. During his sojourn in the city he wrote regularly for the Tribune, Sun, and Mail, as well as doing occasional work for the Brooklyn Eagle, Albany Argus, and several of the many weekly journals published in Gotham.

In the early May days of 1874 Wilkins returned to Whitehall, and his first love, the Times, became his property. Since that time he has been its editor and proprietor, and has made for it a name that takes first rank among the newspapers of America made famous by their humorous paragraphs.

Mr. Wilkins has a wife, two children, and a charming home. Of his family he says: "None of my relatives have ever been hung, but once a brother-in-law came near going to Congress. My war record is good—as during the rebellion I did not have a hand in the public treasury, but a second cousin of my wife sent a substitute, who by jumping bounties like a true patriot, covered the family with glory enough to reach me."

As a politician, Mr. Wilkins succeeded through the aid of his paper and his friends, in holding one office, three times being collector of canal tolls at the port of Whitehall, during the years 1874, 1875,

and 1878.   He is a very small man, being something like five feet four inches in height.   He possesses a pleasant cheery face, and adorns the lower
portion of it with a moustache of a heavy and a
beard of a light growth.   His literary work has of
late years been devoted almost exclusively to
the Times.   Recently he has essayed domestic
sketches, stories of the home circle, and romantic
tales of travel and adventure.

A New York humorist says admiringly of Wilkins: "He is a trump card in the fraternity he
adorns.   Never a stone has he laid in the path
of an earnest fellow laborer.   Meet him when
you will and where you will, there is the same
cordial impressment, the same hand-grip that
goes straight to your marrow of susceptibility.
It has been my lot to meet him when convivi-
ality held full sway, and again when family afflic-
tion had tightly drawn the chords of sympathy;
but the same gentle spirit was the thrall.   The
world is better for such lives; better for the kindly
sentiments that emanate from minds charged less
with self-opinion than liberal thoughts of and for
mankind; better for the outflow of their broad
religion, and safer because it is a religion of impulse, a creed born of sentiment and fostered by
philanthrophy."

Wilkins' admirable essay on Father Adam is

undoubtedly the best thing he has written. It was originally published in the Whitehall Times in 1879, and is as follows:

ADAM'S FALL.

Adam was the first man—if he had been a shoe-maker he would have been the last man.

He was 'placed in the Garden of Eden and was himself the guardian of Eden. He consequently had no partner to order him up mornings, and he, therefore, played it alone.

All the clothes he had for a long time was the close of day, while a mantle of night was his bed-clothes.

He had dominion over the fish of the sea, the birds of the air, and he also had hoe-minion over the earth.

He was finally furnished with a woman of A-rib-ia, who was sent to Eden for Adam's Express Company. She was bone of his beauin', and if she had been called Nancy, she would have been his bone-nancy.

She was a pretty good cook, for she soon cooked up trouble for Adam, and got him into hot water.

When Adam went down to his office mornings, Eve always went to her household duties; but she was a fortunate woman in one respect; she had no washing to do on Monday, so Adam was never afflicted by being obliged to eat mush and milk from the clock-shelf.

Eve never called him back and told him to send home some soap and starch at once, nor did it cost Adam five shillings a week for clothes pins, for the beautiful smile that Mr. and Mrs. Adam always wore could be licked clean with the tip ends of their tongues.

But they were not a happy couple, for the Fourth of July was unknown to Eden.

They never listened to the bang of the cannon, the gun, or the fire-cracker, but Eve used to bang her hair quite often.

Adam never
- wore tight boots.
- had
  - corns.
  - shirts with buttons off.
  - holes in his stockings.
  - holes in his pockets.
- wore patched pantaloons.
- spilt ice cream on his lavender pants.
- pawned his ulster.
- pulled down his vest.
- burst his suspender buttons.
- paid $2 per day for washing.
- owed his tailor.

Eve never
- wore
  - corsets.
  - striped stockings.
  - rats.
  - mice.
  - frizzes.
- was bothered to find a dressmaker.
- found fault with her milliner.
- gossiped with her next door neighbor.
- went to church and made fun of a rival's new bonnet.
- had beaux from church.

When we say never, no one need say hardly

ever.   But Mr. and Mrs. Adam fell just the same. As we draw a veil over their fall, let us ask every head of a family, if he doesn't feel like howling when he remembers that Adam didn't know what a good thing he had

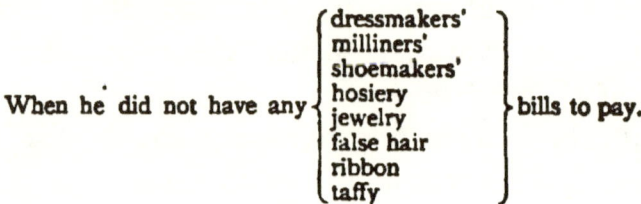

When he did not have any { dressmakers' milliners' shoemakers' hosiery jewelry false hair ribbon taffy } bills to pay.

But he could have laid in his hammock from sunrise to sunset, and read the daily papers without feeling that he must go down town and work like thunder, so his wife and daughters could all have new bonnets to wear to church on next Sabbath day.

Adam was a queer duck and the fathers of to-day owe him a sockdologer.

CHARLES H. HARRIS.

"Carl Pretzel" is a name generally known throughout the West and Northwest. It is the literary sobriquet of Mr. Charles H. Harris, of Chicago, Illinois. He was born in the city of Rochester, New York, on the 20th day of May, 1841. His father was a well-known politician of the Empire State, and Charles, having a living example of the New York State politician constantly before him, resolved at an early age not to enter politics—at least not in New York State. After receiving a common-school education, and passing his early youth at home, Mr. Harris went to New York city in 1862. He was accompanied by other youngsters of his native town.

Harris shipped as a landsman in the navy, and soon after was transferred to the navy yard at Washington, where, in a few months after his arrival, he received the appointment of captain's clerk. He was promoted to the position of paymaster's clerk, and did service on the Potomac river during his one year term of enlistment.

After the war he came home, and after remaining a very short time in Rochester, he set out to seek his fortune.

The oil fever having broken out at this time, Harris was one of the first to become afflicted. He started for Pennsylvania, and became interested in oil wells and oil territory. To use his own words, ''he made a barrel of money, and left it there, it being too cumbersome to carry home.'' In speaking of himself, Harris says: ''In 1866 I was notified that an appointment awaited me in Wyoming Territory, that of Secretary of the Territory. I started at once to grasp the prize. Arriving in Chicago, I learned that my next friend, who had been nominated for Governor of the Territory, did not have friends enough in the Senate to ratify his nomination, consequently his failure to secure the Governorship settled me.''

Harris was left in Chicago like a stranded ship. He embarked into journalism soon after his arrival, and began inflicting the public with ''Pretzelisms,'' by ''Carl Pretzel.'' These consisted of short and witty paragraphs in broken German dialect. They took well, and Harris has made a national reputation through them. He says: ''I began the 'Pretzelisms' to get even with the world, and I will not let up on them.''

For a number of years Mr. Harris has issued

his annual almanac, which has commanded a large and ready sale. A few years ago he issued his first book, "My Book of Expressions," which has had a wide circulation. It contained only articles in the Dutch dialect. The Almanac for 1882, written by Mr. Harris, is overflowing with his peculiar humor, and another large volume, "My Book of Parodies," will soon appear.

"Carl Pretzel," outside of his book work, is a thorough and hard-working journalist. He is at present engaged in editing and publishing a weekly newspaper at 119 Clark street, Chicago. "The National Weekly is eight years old," says Harris in a private letter, "and is a healthy, growing enterprise."

Here is one of Càrl's best small efforts:

"One nite time I comed me home on mine house, und dook mine leedle daughter, Gretchen, Jr., on mine kneeses. I told her some shtory riddles, und vas make her some lafe. Pooty gwick she vas creeb on my bosom, und vas so shleepy, I dook her on her leedle ped, und say of her:

"'Gretchy, would you gone on vour ped mitout saiding your prayers?'

"She opened dem beautiful leedle blue eyses, und radder dreamily exclaimed:

> 'Now I vas lay me down to shleep,
> I pray der——'

dhen adding in one shweet leedle vhisper, 'He knows der rest,' she sunk down on her leedle ped, in His watchful care, who gifs His belofed shleeb."

JOEL CHANDLER HARRIS.

"Uncle Remus" is a well-known character throughout the South, and his fame has even found its way northward. "Uncle Remus" is the literary nickname adopted by Mr. Joel Chandler Harris, a well-known journalist·of the South.   He was born in Eatonton, Georgia, on the 8th of December, 1846.   At a very early age he was taken out of school, and placed at work as "printer's devil" in the office of a country newspaper.

Charles Pilsbury, in a recent article, says of Harris : "He must have had access to many books, and those of the best sort, and he mastered them thoroughly.   One can readily imagine him pursuing his studies in some shady nook in the summer time, and in the winter evenings by the blaze of pine knots or the modest tallow dip.   It was in these days and evenings, we may be sure, that he · obtained the insight into negro character, which has enabled him to portray in 'Uncle Remus,' the *ante bellum* negro."

In 1866 Mr. Harris became connected wih at

publishing house at New Orleans, and he had plenty of spare time to devote to literature. He has written a good deal for southern periodicals, during the last five years; essays, sketches and lyrics have appeared from his pen that would have done honor to older heads. In January, 1867, he published in the New Orleans Times, a poem entitled The Sea Wind, which has been greatly admired.

He returned to Eatonton, Georgia, in May, 1867, where he wrote many articles in both prose and verse. In 1868 Mr. Harris was in Forsythe, Georgia, still bent on following literature as a profession. In June of the same year he was working at the case, and thought some of going to New York, to seek his fortune and a name. About this time he received the promise of an editorial position on a paper about to be established at Savannah, Georgia; and on the 12th of July he writes to a friend that he "thinks he was cut out for a paragraphing journalist."

His newspaper promise failed to realize anything for him, however, and in October he was still at the case in a country newspaper office, longing for journalistic life in a great city. Two years later we find his hopes realized, and Mr. Harris became the associate editor of the Savannah Morning News. He worked hard, and soon placed his name high in rank among Georgia journalists.

After six years of work on the Morning News, Harris purchased an interest in the Atlanta Constitution, and immediately joined its editorial staff. It was in the columns of the Constitution that Uncle Remus and his quaint humor first appeared. From this time forward his success has been rapid, and he has placed his name in the front rank among American humorists. Last year Mr. Harris published his first book, Uncle Remus; His Songs and Sayings. The work took wonderfully well with the public and has had an immense sale.

Of the later works of Uncle Remus, the following are very popular:

PLANTATION PROVERBS.

Drive out de dreamin' dog.

Mighty few horses fits a barley hatch.

Noddin' nigger gives the ash-cake a chill.

Don't fall out wid de fat what cook de 'possum.

Fightin' nigger ain't far from de callaboose.

Ole cloze better go 'round de picket fence.

You kin sell mo' patter rallers dan boozerbears.

Short stirrups en a do'-back horse.

Mighty good sheep w'ats wuff mo' dan his wool.

Sunday pra'rs ain't gwineter las' all de week.

Lazy folks got too many ter-morrers ahead of um.

Don't hol' yo' head too high, less you gwineter eat out'n de hoss-rack.

Hotter de wedder, de fresher de nigger. Dis w'at save de salt.

One eye on de overseer en t'er on de mule don't make de furrer straight.

De shote w'at stays out in der dark er de moon, done gone from home fer good.

Some marsters gotter be tuck on trus'. How de wurm git in de scaly-bark? Who raised de row twixt de bee-martin en de buzzard?

A PLANTATION BALLAD.

I.

De boss, he squall ter de rompin' boys:
Don't bodder dat jug in de spring !
De jug, he guzzle out *good, good, good !*
Nigger, he holler en sing:
Oh, gimme de gal, de big greasy gal
W'at wrap up 'er ha'r wid a string!

II.

Little bird flutter w'en de big speckle hawk
Sail up en light in de pine;
W'en de overseer come en look thro de fence
Nigger don't cut no shine,
But he roll up he eye, en he break loose en sing:
En I wish dat big gal 'us mine!

III.

Oh, de speckle hawk light in de top ob de pine,
En dar he set en swing;

De overseer lean his chin on de fence,
    En lissen at de cotton-choppers sing :
Don't nobody bodder dat sway-back gal
    W'at wrap up 'er ha'r wid a string!

IV.

Oh, de strappin' black gal, de big greasy gal!
    She kyar herse'f mighty fine !
How de boys gwineter foller along in de row,
    A-waitin' for ter ketch her sign ?
De boss mighty close, yet I study en I wish—
    En I wish dat big gal uz mine!

[The italics seem to mark what may be called the refrain choruses. The variable nature of these gives unexpected coloring—not to say humor—to the songs in which they occur. Any typographical arrangement of these choruses must be, in the very nature of things, awkward and ineffective.]

DAVID ROSS LOCKE.

"David Ross Locke, an American satirist," says the American Encyclopedia, yet Locke is a newspaper humorist of the modern school. True, he does not subject himself to the painful necessity of forcing humorous paragraphs into the world, neither is he given to punning. Yet throughout his writing is easily distinguished a dry, uncertain, yet entertaining humor.

David Ross Locke was born in Broome county, New York, in or near the village of Vestal, on the 20th day of September, 1833. After a common school education, lasting but a year or two, young Locke, in 1844, or when he was but eleven years of age, became apprenticed to a printer in Cortland, a few miles distant from Vestal. Learning his trade, he sought out, Bohemian-like, to seek his fortune. He drifted around the country, North and South, varying the occupation with which he earned his daily bread. At different times he acted in the capacity of compositor, reporter and general writer for various newspapers and magazines.

It was in 1852 that young Locke settled down for the first time, at Plymouth, Ohio, where he became connected with the Advertiser, a weekly village newspaper, with a few hundreds circulation. Locke afterwards removed his talents to the Herald, at Mansfield, Ohio ; then he drifted into the offices of the Journal at Bucyrus, Bellefontaine Republican, and the Jeffersonian, a prosperous weekly published at Findlay. It was during his connection with the last named paper that Locke wrote for the Journal, an article signed by the "Rev. Petroleum Vesuvius Nasby." The letter purported to have come from an ignorant and penniless bourbon Democrat, who resided in Kentucky. This character was apparently devoted entirely to free whisky, perpetual, slavery, and a position as postmaster. The letter was dated "Confederit Cross Roads," and soon after its appearance created considerable comment.

Not long after the appearance of the first Nasby letter, Locke changed his location once more, and turned up in the office of the Blade, at Toledo. Here he came to stay. He has stayed there ever since; has grown up with the Blade, and now owns and controls the paper. The "Nasby" letters have made both the Blade and Locke famous all over the country. In a private letter to the writer, Nasby says: "I have kept up the letters ever since 1860, for which I ask forgiveness." At the close of the war Locke, like others of his class, entered the lecture field for a short time, and lectured in nearly all the Northern States. His first volume of letters appeared in 1865, in Cincinnati, under the title of Divers Views, Etc. In 1867 appeared another volume of Nasby letters, published in Boston, under the title of Swingin' Round the Cirkle." In 1868, appeared a third volume, Ekkoes From Kentucky, and, in 1874, a Boston house published his Morals of Abou ben Adhem. This was followed by A Paper City, published by Lee & Shepard, Boston, and Hannah Jane, a poem. This last-named work has had a large sale, and is quite popular. Of this work a leading critic said: "It is certainly one of the best things the Rev. P. V. Nasby ever produced. It has the extraordinary attraction of being in popular and excellent verse. It is real life, and true nature. It touches a chord that will vibrate everywhere; a subject near the heart of many, and in the experience of all. It touches it with honesty, frankness, and self-condemnation, that stings with conviction while it thrills with admiration." One is fully convinced of these facts after a careful perusal of Hannah Jane. The following is a fragment from the poem:

" I was but little better. True, I'd longer been at school;
My tongue and pen were run, perhaps, a trifle more by rule;
But that was all: the neighbors round, who knew us thro' and thro',
Spoke but the truth in calling her the better of the two.

" She blundered in her writing, and she blundered when she spoke,
And ev'ry rule of syntax that old Murray made she broke;
But she was fresh and beautiful, and I——well, I was young;
Her form and face far, far outweighed the blunders of her tongue."

In 1881 Mr. Locke, with his eldest son, sailed for
Europe, where they travelled for nearly a year.
On his return he began a series of papers in the
Toledo Blade, entitled "Nasby in Exile." These
letters were afterwards, in 1882, published in book
form by the Locke Publishing Co., of Toledo,
under the same title. The work is principally descriptive of travel in Ireland, England and on the
Continent. Locke is the author of two plays, "In-
flation" and "Widow Bedott." The last named
has proved very successful, financially and otherwise.

" Nasby" was married to a very estimable lady,
upwards of twenty-six years ago, and is the proud
father of three children. He lives in a quiet, but
elegant manner in the city of Toledo, and is considerably engrossed with the business interests of
the city. Under his able management the weekly
Toledo Blade has become one of the leading
family papers of the country, and circulates in
every State and Territory of the Union. Locke

writes solely for his paper, even his most successful books being made up of material taken from
the columns of the Toledo newspaper.

ROBERT JONES BURDETTE.

The famous funny man of the Burlington, Iowa, Hawkeye, was born at Greensboro, Pennsylvania, on the 30th of July, 1844. At the early age of seven months he went West with his parents, to grow up with the country. They settled in Peoria, Illinois, where at the age of eighteen Robert enlisted as a private, in 1862, in the Forty-seventh Illinois Infantry. He served through the war as a private, was present at the siege of Vicksburg, and was a member of the famous Red River expedition. He showed himself to be a brave and fearless man on various occasions, especially at the battle of Corinth.

Robert J. Burdette, at the close of the war found life's struggle rather severe. He was the oldest son of a family of nine, and aided them as best he could. In after years he made the remark: "As the oldest son I saw it was my duty to help pull the others through." His facilities for acquiring an academic education were limited, and his ambition to enter college has never been gratified.

While on a visit to New York he penned several letters from that city to the Peoria Transcript, and the publication of these letters betrayed his natural inclination for the journalistic life. Upon his return to Peoria he secured a position as proof-reader on the Transcript. In the meantime he wrote numerous sketches for the different New York magazines, but few of which were published or even accepted.

Burdette says of his life from this time forward: "After a while I started a paper of my own—the Peoria Review. I ran it two years. It was a comforting sort of a paper. It brought to me a few cares but no uncertainty. I knew every Monday morning that on the next Saturday night I would not have money enough to pay the hands. During my career as editor of that wretched sheet it never disappointed me in that particular—not once. Finally the sheriff took me into partnership, and there was a glorious increase of activity. He was an enterprising man, very. He realized more in an hour than I had done in two years. Presently the partnership dissolved, and I looked around for something to do. I thought I would try and get on the Burlington Hawkeye. It was a sober, staid old paper, financially solid. I was young and active. Thought I, 'I think I can do that paper good. If I can get on the staff I am

sure it will do me good. Well, I was thinking of
going over there when one day its manager, Mr.
Wheeler, came to see me, and offered me the position of city editor and reporter. Well, if I live
ten thousand years it will not be long enough time
for me to be sufficiently thankful that I accepted
the offer, and, besides that, I am very proud of the
fact that they sent for me. It gave me an inde-
pendence of personal satisfaction that I have never
recovered from. I don't try to be funny in my
writings. I have an idea, occasionally, and when
I get it loose people 'laugh. Then I review the
remark and shake it out to find the fun. My per-
ception of a joke is not hung on a hair trigger."

In 1870, Mr. Burdette became affianced to Miss
Carrie Garrett, of Peoria, Illinois. She was a frail
and delicate young lady, and on visiting her one
afternoon, Robert was met at the door by her
friends, who announced that she was lying at the
point of death. The situation was a grave one, but
in fifteen minutes' time he had procured a marriage
license from the county clerk's office, and Miss
Garrett became Mrs. Robert J. Burdette at a time
when her responses could only be made by a slight
motion of the eyes and a faint pressure of the
hand. But little hope was entertained for her life,
but she passed the ordeal, and after some length
of time rallied sufficiently to go with her husband

on a short bridal tour to their quiet home in a neighboring street, in Peoria. Mrs. Burdette has been an invalid all her life, and the genial humorist has been a patient attendant and companion for her in her dreary hours of life. The major portion of the rollicking humor that Burdette produces, is written at the bed side of his invalid wife.

It was soon after his marriage, when he was doing editorial work on the Peoria Transcript, that Burdette began his humorous writing. 'He tells of it in his own words as follows: " When I was on the Transcript, I would try to think of something pleasant to tell the folks when I went home at night—something that would make a tea-table lively. And when nothing of a funny nature occurred, I would make up something, such as one of the burlesques concerning the Middle Rib Family. They seemed to be enjoyed around the tea-table, and finally Mrs. Burdette urged me to write them up. I told her that they would sound as flat as dish-water in print—that it was nothing but tea-table chatter, and that she must not be so highly impressed by my nonsense. But she persisted, and so I would occasionally write in a light vein for the Transcript. The sketches seemed to take, and then I plunged into deep water." Afterwards Burdette said of his humor: "You see, I don't know how I do say things people think funny, and sometimes I am in a state of mind bordering on insanity to know why people think they are so. I certainly had no school except the wide world, from which to learn the lesson of fun; and, now I come to think of it, perhaps the page was the most instructive that could have been placed before me."

From 1874 to the date of his joining the editorial corps of the Burlington Hawkeye, Mr. Burdette rose rapidly as a humorist, and after his writings and the Hawkeye both had become famous, he entered-the lecture field. His first lecture was decided upon and written by the promptings of his wife. This little episode Robert tells as follows: "One day when she was lying helpless, she said she believed that I could write a lecture and deliver it successfully, and so she sat me down to write that lecture; and from time to time I rebelled with tears and groans and prayers. I told her that I was too little, that I had no voice, that I couldn't write a funny lecture, anyhow. She kept me at it, and in due time we had a lecture on our hands:—'The Rise and Fall of the Mustache.' That was all right enough; now how to get the audience. I thought I would try it first at Keokuk. If I delivered it first in Burlington, even though it were tame, tamer, tamest, I thought they might pat me on the back. But

Keokuk hated Burlington. I thought that if it was flat the Keokuk folks would tell me so. Mrs. Burdette said that, as she was responsible for that lecture, she was going to hear it first delivered. So I carried her aboard the cars. We went down to Keokuk, and they pronounced it good."

The whole of the United States have since agreed with Keokuk. Burdette has lectured in about every State in the Union to delighted audiences. Taking his age into consideration, Mr. Burdette is very youthful in appearance. He is short in stature, easy in manner, and affable in conversation. He has a low, broad forehead, a black mustache, rounded chin, and dark, yet bright, penetrating eyes. When writing at any considerable length, he scarcely ever has a definite plan for his effusion, and lets it take its own free way from the point of his pen. He has written much in verse and prose, but his humorous descriptions and pen pictures of those he meets in every-day life, are the most readable of his productions. It is natural for him to be funny, and in speaking of the most common-place things he expresses himself in the most humorous way.

Burdette has published two books: The Rise and Fall of the Mustache, and Hawkeye Glances, both volumes commanding a large sale. He has written much for the literary weeklies, and his pen is never idle.   Among his attempts and successes in poetry nothing equals his touching tribute to

WILHELMJ.

> Oh, king of the fiddle, Wilhelmj,
> If truly you love me, just tellmj;
>   Just answer my sigh
>   By the glance of your eye,
> Be honest, and don't try to sellmj.
>
> With rapture your music did thrillmj;
> With pleasure supreme did it fillmj,
>   And if I could believe
>   That you meant to deceive—
> Wilhelmj, I think it would killmj.

Among the thousand and one "good things" that Burdette has given us, none contains more of his genuine, characteristic humor than his

NIGHT THOUGHTS.

Don't judge a man by his clothes. Can you tell what the circus is going to be like by looking at the Italian sunset pictures on the fence? Do you value the turkey for its plumage? And isn't the skin of the mink the most, and, indeed, the only valuable part of him? There be men, fair to look upon, who wander up and down this country, and sit in the coolest places on the hotel piazzas, who are arrayed in fine linen and cardinal socks, and who have to hold their hand over their scarf-pin when they want to see the moonlight, who, unassisted and unprompted, do not possess

the discretion to come in when it rains, and don't
know enough to punch a hole in the snow with an
umbrella—new, soft snow at that, without any
crust on it.   Now and then, son, before you are
as old as Methuselah, you will meet a man who
wears a hat that is worth twice as much as the
head it covers.   On the other hand, don't fall into
the error of believing that all the goodness, and
honesty, and intelligence in the world goes about
in shreds and patches.   We have seen the tramp
dressed in worse rags than you could rake out of
the family rag-bag, and more dirt and hair on him
than would suffice to protect a horse, who would
step up to the front door and demand three kinds
of cake, half an apple pie, and then steal every
moveable thing in the yard, kill the dog, choke up
the pump with sand, tramp on the pansy bed and
girdle the cherry trees, because he couldn't carry
them away.   Good clothes or bad are never an
infallible index to a man that is in them.

JOE C. ABY.

The subject of this sketch is a resident of New Orleans. His entire life, almost, has been spent there. His name,—that of Aby,—is an uncommon one and a short one, and with the short, very short, surname of Joe prefixed, makes the whole an extraordinary short name. Joe C. Aby has written much in the way of humor, under the rather curious name of "Hoffenstein." The larger portion of his productions have appeared in the way of sketches, in the columns of that well known Southern newspaper, the New Orleans Times-Democrat.

Joe C. Aby was born on the 23d day of July, 1858, and is consequently one of the youngest of our American humorists. According to his own story, he was in boyhood "a tame sort of individual. I was not vicious, nor was I given to saying smart things, for the reason that my father, whose kindly hand is now still in death, had a habit of hovering around the rear portion of my anatomy with a strap, in order to impress upon my tender mind the fact that it was not becoming in a small boy to get 'too big for his old clothes.' His theory was, that the seat of a boy's pants was the proper medium through which to reach the mind, and the demonstrations of his theory were invariably successful.

"My school life was not at all remarkable, or different from that of the average urchin. It consisted of thrashings, which I received from the pedagogue for not knowing my lessons. He was a man who clung to the motto: 'Hit for the basement, let the rod fall where it may;' but even while he was doing so, I felt that there was a destiny that would model my end, despite his efforts to hammer it out of shape. At the age of fourteen years I entered a collegiate institute, but at sixteen, my career there was abruptly terminated by the right boot of the principal, who foolishly believed that a student deserved immediate expulsion, who was bold enough to attempt to punch the head of a German professor. After my hasty exit from college, I migrated to Texas for the benefit of my health.

"For seven or eight years I lived among the cattle ranches in the southwestern portion of the Lone Star State. While in Texas I drifted around promiscuously from one kind of business to another, until a position was offered me, as a reporter, on the local staff of the Houston Daily Post—a journalistic venture which has since proved a success, and is now a leading paper in Texas. I made my appearance as a journalist with the first issue of the paper. During my sojourn on the staff of the paper, I dabbled somewhat in humorous writing, which attracted some attention. Finally, I received an offer from the New Orleans Times to join its staff of writers. This offer I accepted at once, and returned to my native city. I remained with the Times until its consolidation with the New Orleans Democrat was effected, when I was offered a position on the local staff of the hyphenated journal—The Times-Democrat. This offer I also accepted, and have since served that paper."

Under the *nom de plume* of "Hoffenstein," Mr. Aby has written much that is not only funny, but ridiculously so. His Hoffenstein sketches in the Times-Democrat have won for him a national reputation, and his writings are reproduced in papers in various parts of the country. He is a young man, unmarried, handsome and dignified. A volume of the Hoffenstein sketches has been issued by a New York publishing house, and has been flattered by a ready sale.

One of the most popular of these sketches is the following·

THERMOMETER PANTS.

Hoffenstein was busily engaged scolding Hermann for not polishing a lot of brass jewelry there was in a show case, when a thin, stoop-shouldered countryman entered the store and inquired:

"Have you got any good jean pants here?"

"Certainly, my frent," replied Hoffenstein, "ve makes a specialty uf goods in dot line, und ve defy competition. If ve sells anyding und you don't lik it, you gets your money back or someding else in exshange, you know. Vas you a farmer?"

"Yes, sir, I live up on Red River."

"Vell, den, you need a bair uf bants like dese," said Hoffenstein, pulling out a sky-blue pair from a pile of clothing on the counter. "Dey vas de genervine doeskin, und will last de whole year oud."

The countryman took the pants to the light, examined the texture of the cloth, and then shaking his head knowingly said:

"There's too much cotton in them; they will shrink."

"Of course my frent dey will shrink, but vait und I tells you someding. If a man vat owns a pank or keeps a store comes here, I don't sell him dem kind uf pants. Vy? Because dey vas made exbressly for de farming pisiness. Dey vas de dermometer pants, und a plessing to every farmer vat vears a bair uf dem. Do you know, my frent, dose bants vill dell you exactly vat de vedder will be. Ven it vas going to be vet and cold, dose bants vill begin to shrink up, und ven it vas going to be dry und varm, dey comes right down, you know. Dree years ago, I sell a bair of dem to a man vat vas named Vilking, und eber since den he makes good crops, ven de oder beoble don't make noding, because he always knows py his dermometer pants vat de vedder vill be. After avile de beoble in de neighborhood finds oud de segret uf Vilkin's success, and at the beginning of the planting season, you know, dey comes for dirty miles around, and if dey see Vilkin's bants crawling up his leg dey holds off und vaits for a change, but if his bants vas down dey goes right back home, und puts in de crop. Dink of it, my frent ; mit de thermometer bants, you can tell exactly ven to put in cabbage seed, und plant corn twice as better as mit an almanac, besides ven de vedder gets so cold und vet dot de bants goes up under your arms, you sew buttons on the front and vear him as a vest."

When Hoffenstein finished his yarn concerning the pants, the countryman smiled, and, turning abruptly on his heel, left the store.

"Did you see de vay dot my acted, Her-mann?" said Hoffenstein, angrily.

"Yes, sir," replied his clerk.

"Vell, it shust shows dot de more you dry to help beoble along, de more, py tam, you don't got any tanks for it."

EDWARD E. EDWARDS.

The subject of this sketch is known but little, although his humor has acquired fame widespread and universal. Edward E. Edwards is the paragrapher and "funny man" of the Boston Transcript. This journal has become famous for its bright and racy column of "Facts and Fancies," and for the hundreds of sparkling humorous sketches that have appeared in its columns during a great number of years.

Edward E. Edwards, the life of the journal, is a New Englander. Born and reared in the vicinity of the great metropolis of culture, Edwards has become one of the institutions of Boston. While yet a youth he entered into the employ of the Transcript, in the capacity of assistant in the mailing-room in the basement. He worked steadily; and gradually, as he became a man, ascended in the business he had chosen, step by step, until he now holds a remunerative position in the editorial rooms on the fifth floor of the Transcript building.

Edwards is the fortunate possessor of a vein of

humor of very peculiar composition, and he occupies in the world of wit a field entirely his own. The column of bright paragraphs published under the caption of Facts and Fancies has long been one of the leading features of the Boston Transcript, and is widely quoted. Edwards has made his most happy hits, however, in his descriptive sketches, lectures to the young, etc., that have appeared in his paper. These have been more widely copied, perhaps, than any one class of humorous sketches that have appeared in this country during the last decade. Their author is a small man, of good appearance, weighing one hundred and sixty pounds, and is about six and thirty years of age.

As a fair specimen of the humor that springs from the pen of Edwards, I annex the following discourse to little children on

THE EDITOR.

The editor is a member of that race of animals called mankind. He is invariably a kind man.

He is perfectly harmless. You may go into his den without fear. But he has his peculiarities. The sight of a poet makes him wild. He is then very dangerous, and is apt to do bodily harm to all within his reach. He is also wrought up when a man comes in with a little trifle he has just dashed off.

There is one thing that must be said in the editor's dispraise. His mind is so biased by long thinking in a certain direction, that he dislikes very much to look upon both sides of a question. Therefore, if you value your safety, never approach him with manuscript written on both sides of your paper. Let me say right here, children, that a good deal of sheer nonsense has been written about the editor. He uses his shears only when composing an entirely original article. He usually writes with his pen, but his most cutting articles are the product of his shears.

The editor would make a good public speaker but for his propensity for clipping words. The editor's hardest task is to dispose of his time. It is a monotonous life, indeed, were it not for the kindness of the few hundred people who call upon him every day, to enliven his dull life with stories of their grievances, of their new enterprises and with antediluvian anecdotes.

When you grow up to be men and women, children, remember this, and spend all the time you can in the sanctum of the editor. He loves company so much, you know, and sometimes he has to sit silent alone for a whole half minute. Is it not too bad? The business of the editor is to entertain itinerant lecturers, book canvassers, exchange fiends, and other philanthropists. He gives his whole day to these. He writes his editorials at night after he has gone to bed.

The editor is never so happy as when he is writing complimentary notices. For ten cents worth of presents he will gladly give ten dollars worth of advertising—all on account of the pleasure it gives him to write, you know, children. He loves to write neat little speeches and bright, witty poems for people without brains, who wish to speak in public. It is so easy to do this that he is sometimes quite miserable when an hour or two passes without an opportunity to do something of the kind.

The editor dines at all the hotels free, he travels free, theaters open wide their doors to him, the tailor clothes him gratis, his butcher and grocer furnish him with food without money and without price. In short, his every want is provided for. He spends his princely salary in building churches and school-houses in foreign lands.

By all means, children, be editors. Of course, it would be better if you could be hod-carriers or dray horses, but, as that is impossible, by all means be editors.

EUGENE FIELD.

One of the most clever of Western humorists is Eugene Field. He is a native of Missouri, having been born in St. Louis, September 2, 1850. His mother died when he was but six years of age, and he was sent, with a younger brother, to Amherst, Massachusetts, and placed under the care of his cousin, Miss French. He was fitted for college by the Rev. James Tufts, of Monson, and entered Williams college in 1868. Upon the death of his father, in 1869, he returned to the West, and has since then made his home on the western side of the Mississippi. He left the State University of Missouri at the close of his junior year, and went to Europe, where he remained for seven months.

In 1873 Mr. Field became a reporter on the St. Louis Evening Journal, of which paper Stanley Huntley (now of the Brooklyn Eagle) was then city editor. He changed his location soon after to St. Joseph, where for eighteen months he was associate editor of the St. Joseph Gazette.

He then moved to Kansas City, where, for a
period of twenty months, he acted as managing
editor of the Daily Times.   He was with the St.
Louis Times-Journal during its best days, and was
twice elected poet of the Missouri Press Association. He is, at the present writing, managing editor
of the Denver Tribune.   He has been married
eight years and is the father of four living children.

It was in 1878 that Mr. Field first began writing verse, and, for a young poet, his productions
were highly complimented.   His first effort was
a little poem of ten stanzas, which was printed in
a St. Louis paper.   It was entitled :

THE CHRISTMAS TREASURES.

I count my treasures o'er with care—
   A little toy that baby knew—
   A little lock of faded hue—
A little lock of golden hair.

Long years ago this Christmas time,
   My little one—my all to me—
   Sat, robed in white, upon my knee,
And heard the Merry Christmas chime.

"Tell me, my little golden-head,
   If Santa Claus should come to-night,
   What shall he bring my baby bright—
What treasure for my boy?" I said.

And then he named the little toy,
   While in his round and truthful eyes
   There came a look of glad surprise
That spoke his trustful, childish joy.

And as he lisped his evening pray'r,
　　He asked the boon with baby grace,
　　And toddling to the chimney place,
He hung his little stocking there.

That night, as length'ning shadows crept,
　　I saw the white-winged angels come
　　With music to our humble home
And kiss my darling as he slept.

They must have heard his baby pray'r,
　　For in the morn, with glowing face,
　　He toddled to the chimney place
And found the little treasure there.

They came again one Christmas tide—
　　That angel host, so fair and white—
　　And, singing all the Christmas night,
They lured my darling from my side.

A little sock, a little toy—
　　A little lock of golden hair—
　　The Christmas music on the air—
A watching for my baby boy.

But if again that angel train
　　And golden-head come back for me,
　　To bear me to eternity,
My watching will not be in vain.

Other efforts in a similar vein followed, of which the following is a fair sample:

THE PRAYER.

Long years have passed since that sweet time
　　When first I breathed upon the air
　　My simple little baby prayer—
A prayer with earnestness sublime;
Since first my mother clasped my hands,
　　And bade me, ere I went to sleep,

Pray God my little soul to keep,
Or take to dwell in heav'nly land.

And now, tho' years on years have fled,
    And tho' the mother's passed away,
    And tho' my head be bowed and gray,
The little prayer that then I said
Comes floating back on angel wing,
    As if, upon the other shore,
    A little child had lisped it o'er
For God's own messengers to bring.

His work in a lighter vein is fairly represented by the following:

THE SAME DEAR HAND.

The bells ring out a happy sound,
    The earth is mantled o'er with white,
    It is the merry Christmas night,
And love and mirth and joy abound.
And here sit you and here sit I;
    I should be happiest in the land,
    For, oh, I hold the same dear hand
I've held for many a year gone by!

It is not withered up with care;
    It is as fresh and fair to see,
    As sweet to hold and dear to me,
As when with chimes upon the air
On Christmas nights of years ago
    I held the same dear little thing
    And felt its soft caresses bring
The flushes to my throbbing brow.

Ah, we were born to never part!
    This little hand I hold to-night,
    And I, so with a strange delight,
I press it to my beating heart,
And in the midnight's solemn hush
    I bless the little hand I hold.

In broken whispers be it told,
It is the old-time bobtail flush.

Then again in the following:

THE WARRIOR.

Under the window is a man
    Playing an organ all the day—
Grinding as only a cripple can,
    In a moody, vague, uncertain way.

His coat is blue and upon his face
    Is a look of high-born, restless pride—
There is somewhat about him of martial grace
    And an empty sleeve hangs at his side.

"Tell me, warrior, bold and true,
    In what carnage, night or day,
Came the merciless shot to you,
    Bearing your good right arm away?"

Fire dies out in the patriot's eye,
    Changed my warrior's tone and mien—
Choked by emotion, he makes reply—
    "Kansas—harvest—threshing machine."

In October, 1881, Mr. Field commenced the publication of the Denver Tribune Primer, which he abandoned as soon as it began to be generally imitated. Samples of his primer style are appended:

MENTAL ARITHMETIC.

How many Birds are there in Seven soft-boiled Eggs?

If you have Five Cucumbers and eat Three, what will you have Left? Two? No, you are Wrong. You will have More than that. You will have Colic enough to Double you up in a Bow

Knot for Six Hours.   You may go to the Foot of the Class.

A Man had Six Sons and Four Daughters.   If he had had Six Daughters and Four Sons, how many more Sons than Daughters would He have had?

If a Horse weighing 1600 pounds can Haul four tons of Pig Iron, how many Seasons will a Front Gate painted Blue' carry a young Woman on One Side and a young Man on the Other?

THE WASP.

See the wasp.   He has pretty yellow stripes around his Body, and a Darning Needle in his Tail.   If You Will Pat the Wasp upon the Tail, we will Give You a Nice Picture Book.

THE EDITOR'S HOME.

Here is a Castle.   It is the Home of an Editor. It has Stained Glass windows and Mahogany stairways.   In front of the Castle is a Park.   Is it not Sweet?   The lady in the Park is the editor's wife. She wears a Costly robe of Velvet trimmed with Gold Lace, and there are Pearls and Rubies in her Hair.   The editor sits on the front Stoop smoking an Havana Cigar.   His little Children are Playing with diamond Marbles on the Tesselated Floor. The editor can afford to Live in Style   He gets Seventy-Five Dollars a month Wages.

THE SWEET HOME.

Mamma is Larruping Papa with the Mop Handle. The children are Fighting over a Piece of Pie in the Kitchen. Over the Piano there is a Beautiful Motto in a gilt Frame. The Beautiful Motto says there is no Place like Home.

THE CATERPILLAR.

The Caterpillar is Crawling along the Fence. He has Pretty Fur all over his Back, and he Walks by Wrinkling up his Skin. He is Full of Nice yellow Custard. Perhaps you had better take him Into the house, where it is Warm, and Mash him on the Wall Paper with Sister Lulu's Album. Then the Wall Paper will Look as if a Red Headed Girl had been leaning Against it.

THE DIAMOND PIN.

Here is a Diamond Pin. The Editor won it at a Church Fair. There were Ten Chances at Ten Cents a Chance. The Editor Mortgaged his Paper and Took one Chance. The Pin is Worth seven hundred Dollars. Editors like Diamonds. Sometimes they Wear them in their Shirts, but Generally in their Mind.

Eugene Field has written a number of stories, all of a sombre nature. He has at various times been solicited to contribute to Eastern publications, but has steadily declined to do so.

STANLEY HUNTLEY.

"Mr. and Mrs. Spoopendyke" are well-known characters. The exceedingly funny descriptions of the home life of Spoopendyke and his better-half, that first appeared in the columns of the Daily Eagle, of Brooklyn, New York, in 1881, have been reproduced in thousands of newspapers in this country, and in Europe. They are written in a style highly original, and occupy a field entirely their own.

Mr. Stanley Huntley, the author of these lively sketches, is a resident of Brooklyn, and has for years occupied a prominent position in the editorial rooms of the Daily Eagle. He is a born journalist, and has been engaged on many newspapers in both the East and West For many years he was city editor of the St. Louis Evening Journal, and has also held positions on other St. Louis papers. It was not until 1881, early in the year, that Mr. Huntley's humorous writings began to attract the attention of the public. They were so original, so brilliantly witty, and such oddities in

themselves, that the Brooklyn Eagle became famous through their publication. Spoopendyke at
once sprang into popular favor, and the name was
known in every city and village in the country.

During this season of popularity, Mr. Huntley
gathered together his best sketches, and brought
them out in book form through the New York
publishing house of W. B. Smith & Company.
The book sold with a rapidity that was simply
wonderful, and under the simple title of Spoopendyke, over 300,000 copies of the work were
manufactured and disposed of within three months
after its first appearance. Several revised and
enlarged editions have since been published.

Mr. Huntley is of middle age, of lively tem-
perament, pleasing manners, and is kind and sym-
pathetic. He has been married for a number of
years to a handsome and highly cultured lady, and
lives with happy surroundings in a retired street
in Brooklyn. Early in 1882, he was compelled,
by serious illness, to cease his labors for a number
of months.

It is extremely difficult to determine which is
his best production. The Spoopendyke sketches
are all good. Here is a fair specimen of them:

SPOOPENDYKE'S ILLNESS.

" How long have I been in this measly old bar-
racks?" asked Mr. Spoopendyke, turning pain-

fully in his bed, and gazing in a vague, half-dazed way toward a long line of antidotes on the mantel.

"About two weeks, dear," said Mrs. Spoopendyke, coming toward him with a bowl of gruel, and smiling pleasantly. "The doctor says you are not likely to have another attack if you keep very quiet, and follow his instructions."

"Oh, he does, does he?" said Mr. Spoopendyke, making a vain effort to sit up, and falling back with a groan. "He says I won't have another attack? Now, what do you suppose the dod-gasted, bald-pated pill-roller knows about my case, anyway? Perhaps you think he could make an Egyptian mummy dance a Highland fling, and put life into a cigar sign. All he needs is three bulletins a day and unlimited chin to become one of the leading physicians of the country. I suppose if I take all that stuff up there I shall be born again, and see the next centennial. What does that bone-sawing, blistering old ape know about the future, anyway. How can he tell whether I will have another attack or not? Perhaps he will tell you the name of your next husband, and the color of his hair, for fifty cents. Perhaps he is a dod-gasted Spiritualist. What's that?"

"Gruel," said Mrs. Spoopendyke.

"Gruel, always gruel," said Mr. Spoopendyke,

turning his face to the wall. "Do you .magine I'm a Sheltering Arms and St. John's Guild excursion thrown into one? Why don't you tie a bib around my neck, get me a rubber to chew on, and put a rattle in my hand?"

"But the doctor says you must not eat solid food at pres"—

Oh, I'm not to eat solid food," said Mr. Spoopendyke, kicking viciously at the foot-board. "A diet of cannon-balls and scrap-iron won't agree with me. It won't do for me to attempt digesting steel rails and bridge girders. He thinks they won't agree with me, does he? The measly old rattle-brained powder-mixer. Here, give me that stuff," and Mr. Spoopendyke knocked the bowl out of his wife's hands, spilling the contents over the bed-clothes. "There, now I suppose you are satisfied," he said, squirming over toward the wall, and digging his face in the pillow, while Mrs. Spoopendyke gathered up the pieces, and said it was so fortunate that the bowl was only earthenware.

———

The following excellent satire on the current juvenile literature of the day, was originally published in the columns of the Brooklyn Eagle:

INVESTIGATING LIGHT LITERATURE.

The other day a stout woman, armed with an umbrella and leading a small urchin, called at the office of a New York boys' story paper.

"Is this the place where they fight Indians?" she inquired of the gentleman in charge. "Is this the locality where the brave boy charges up the canyon and speeds a bullet to the heart of the dusky red-skin?" and she jerked the urchin around by the ear and brought her umbrella down on the desk.

"We publish stories for boys," replied the young man evasively.

"I want to know if these are the premises on which the daring lad springs upon the fiery mustang and, darting through the circle of thunderstruck savages, cuts the captive's cords and bears him away before the wondering Indians have recovered from their astonishment! That's the information I'm after. I want to know if that sort of thing is perpetrated here!" and she swung the umbrella around her head and launched a crack at the young man's head.

"I don't remember those specific acts," protested the young man.

"I want to know if this is the precinct where the adventurous boy jumps on the back of a buffalo and with unerring aim, picks off one by one, the bloodthirsty pursuers, who bite the dust at every crack of his faithful rifle! I'm looking for the place where that sort of thing happens!" and this time she brought the unlucky young man a tremendous whack across the back.

"I think—?' commenced the dodging victim.

"I'm in search of the shop in which the boy road agent holds the quivering stage driver powerless with his glittering eye, while he robs the male passengers with an adroitness born of long and tried experience, and kisses the hands of the lady passengers with a gallantry of bearing that bespeaks noble birth and a chivalrous nature!" screamed the woman, driving the young man into the corner. "I'm looking for the apartment in which that business is transacted!" and down came the umbrella with trip-hammer force on the young man's head.

"Upon my soul, ma'am—!" gasped the wretched youth.

"I want to be introduced to the jars in which you keep the boy scouts of the Sierras! Show me the bins full of the boy detectives of the prairie! Point out to me the barrels full of boy pirates of the Spanish main!" and with each demand she dropped the umbrella on the young man's skull, until he skipped over the desk and sought safety in a neighboring canyon.

"I'll teach 'em!" she panted, grasping the urchin by the ear and leading him off. "I'll teach 'em to make it good or dance. Want to go fight Indians any more? Want to stand proudly upon the pinnacle of the mountain and scatter the plain beneath with the bleeding bodies of uncounted slain? Want to say 'hist' in a tone that brooks no contradiction? Propose to spring upon the taffrail and with a ringing word of command send a broadside into the richly laden galley, and then mercifully spare the beautiful maiden in the cabin, that she may become your bride? Eh! Going to do it any more?"

With each question she hammered the yelping urchin until his bones were sore and he protested his permanent abandonment of all the glories enumerated.

"Then come along," said she, taking him by the collar. "Let me catch you around with any more ramrods and carving knives, and you'll think the leaping, curling, resistless prairie fire had swept with a ferocious roar of triumph across the trembling plains and lodged in your pantaloons to stay!"

SOME OTHER FUNNY FELLOWS.

There are hundreds of humorists in America who are comparatively unknown—humorists who are intensely funny, but who do not know it; persons who write one or two good things and then cease to write ; journalists of the staid, old school, who once in a decade or so say something really witty.   During the last ten years I have endeavored to accumulate a portion of the many stray bits of fun that have appeared in the American newspapers from time to time.

As an example I quote the following from an unknown humorist: " The editor of a mining camp newspaper went to Denver to hear Emma Abbott sing, and in a review of the opera said : ' As a singer she can just wallop the hose off anything that ever wagged a jaw on the boards. From her clear, bird-like upper-notes, she would canter away down on the base racket and then cushion back to a sort of spiritual treble, which made every man in the audience imagine every hair on his head was the golden string of a celestial harp,

over which angelic fingers were sweeping in the
inspiring old tune, Sallie Put the Kettle on.   Here
she would rest awhile, trilling like an enchanted
bird, and hop in among the upper notes again
with a get-up and-git vivacity that jingled the glass
pendants on the chandeliers, and elicited a whoop
of pleasure from every galoot in the mob.   In the
last act she made a neat play, and worked in that
famous kiss of hers on Castle.   He had her in his
arms with her head lying on his shoulder, and her
eyes shooting red-hot streaks of galvanized love
right into his.   All at once her lips began to
twitch coaxingly and get into position, and
when he tumbled to her racket, he drawed her
up easy like, shut his eyes, and then her ripe,
luscious lips glewed themselves to his and a
thrill of pleasure nabbed hold of him, and shook
him till the audience could almost hear his toe-
nails grind against his boots.   Then she shut her
eyes and pushed harder and dash—O, Moley
Hoses!—the smack that followed started the
stitching in every masculine heart in the house.''

A Montana editor writes as follows of a hated
rival:—''The blear-eyed picture of melancholy
and imbecility who has ravaged his exchanges to
fill up The Insect during the past year, and the
cheerful looking corpse who has acted lately as

his man Friday, and who is a tenderfoot, equally soft at both ends, will doubtless paralyze everybody to-day with his thunderbolts of choice sarcasm and polite invective. The intelligibility of their phillippics, however, will depend largely on whether they could borrow that dictionary or not, their vocabulary being painfully abridged if left to their own resources."

———

The editor of the Solid Muldoon, a weekly journal published at Ouray, Colorado, thus vaunted his own paper: "It is the most powerful antidote for meanness and kindred diseases, ever offered to a suffering community. Elder Ripley, who hasn't told the truth in thirty-two years, feels better, and he has only been on our list two months. Captain Stanley, who hasn't tasted water for thirteen years, can now look at a brooklet without serious results. Ed Snydom, who has been troubled with his spine ever since the Ute outbreak, put out a large washing Monday. Jim Vance, who came to this country with an Arkansas record, now moves in the first society. O, it is a perfect balsam; two-fifty per annum. One annum contains fifty-two doses."

———

An editor in Texas gives the following figures from a statistical memorandum of his life:

Been asked to drink	11,362 times
Drank	11,362 times
Requested to retract	416 times
Didn't retract	416 times
Been invited to parties and receptions by parties fishing for puffs	3,333 times
Took the hint	33 times
Didn't take the hint	3,300 times
Threatened to be whipped	170 times
Been whipped	0 times
Whipped the other fellow	4 times
Didn't come to time	166 times
Been promised whiskey, gin etc., if we would go after them	5,610 times
Been after them	5,610 times
Been asked what's the news	300,000 times
Told	23 times
Didn't know	200,000 times
Lied about it	99,977 times
Been to church	2 times
Changed politics	32 times
Expect to change still	50 times
Gave to charity	$5.00
Gave for terrier dog	$25.00
Cash on hand	$1.00

The following cheerful valedictory of an editor was printed in the Asheville, North Carolina, Journal: "In this issue of the paper I offer my house and lot for sale. My object is to quit the country—possibly for the country's good. For the past nine years I have endeavored to make a livelihood here at the newspaper business, and at this writing I am a good breathing representation of the Genius of Famine, or an allegory of Ireland

during the potato rot.   The day star of my prosperity has gone down behind a dark cloud of
unpaid and uncancelled obligations.   As a dernier
resort, I propose to cast my lot among the Mon-
golians of the Pacific coast, and with this view my
leisure moments are devoted to deciphering the
hieroglyphics on a Chinese tea-chest, while I
patiently await the advent of a purchaser."

———

The following criticism of the acting of Mary
Anderson was written by a Milwaukee, Wisconsin,
journalist: "Mary is about six feet in height when
in repose, but when her frame is charged with
emotion, and she gets mad, or excited, she seems
to rise right up out of the stage and telescope
until she is eighteen or nineteen feet high, and
others look like dwarfs.   At times she puts on a
sweet, lovely look, and you would have to be held
by two persons to keep you from mounting the
stage, and telling her that you loved her like a
steam engine; and then she would put on a dying
look, and a wild, scared, desperate expression, so
you want to rush out after a doctor.   She has
lungs like a blacksmith's bellows; when she
contracts them, she looks so thin that her back
bone can be traced with the naked eye; but when
she inflates them, her dress fits her like paper on
the wall."

Thomas Snell Weaver, the funny man of the New Haven, Connecticut, Register, is one of the coming humorists of the day. He is widely quoted. The following is from his writings:

"There was an extra air of refinement about the front parlor. The storks on a shingle and the Egyptian figures on panels had all been removed to the back parlor to make room for the super-æstheticism of the aureolan glory of the sunflower and the drooping grace of the lily embroidered on bannerets and hung in fitting corners of the grand old room. In this room they sat, and quietly enjoyed each other's presence, bound together by ties yet undiscovered.

"'Angela' said he, 'I think it is four years this very night since we gazed into the firelight together.'

"'So long, Mr. Thistlewaite?' said she tremulously, and in expectant mood.

"'Now, I should think that after so long a time—it occurs to me to say—or rather to ask—why wouldn't it be well—to call me "George" hereafter?'

"'Oh, is that all?' she said. The harpstrings of her expectancy had just been struck with a chord, but alas! the matrimonial overture was not then to be played. The whole orchestra was out of tune for her for the next six weeks.

Mr. H. T. White, a member of the editorial staff of the Chicago Tribune, is also designed to make his mark in the world as a humorist. His style is peculiar, as the following selection will no doubt show:

"'Do not go, darling'—and as she spoke the words—spoke them in low, tender tones, that thrilled him from mail-truck to keelsom—Gwendolen Mahaffey laid her soft, white cheek on Plutarch Riordan's shoulder, and gave him a look with her lustrous, dove-like eyes that would make your head swim.

"'I cannot stay,' he replied, kissing the peachy red lips as he spoke, and feeling wistfully in his overcoat pocket for a plug of tobacco, 'I must go now right away.'

"But the girl placed her arms around his neck—arms whose soft, rounded curves and pink-tinted skin would have made an anchorite throw up his job, and pleaded with him to stay a little longer.

"'I cannot,' he again said, looking at her tenderly.

"'Cannot?' repeated the girl, a shade of anger tinging the tone in which the words were uttered. 'And pray, sir, what is it that so imperatively calls you hence?'

"Bending over her with a careless grace that artfully concealed the slight bagginess at the knees of his pants, Plutarch said, in low, bitter tones that were terrible in their intensity :

"'I have broken my suspenders!'"

———

H. C. Dodge, as a writer of humorous and witty verse, has few equals in America. His style is somewhat like that of the late lamented Tom Hood. One of Mr. Dodge's productions is entitled

CONTRARY MAN.

Some men do write when they do wrong
    And some do live who dye;
And some are short when they are long
    And stand when they do lie.

A man is surly when he's late,
    And round when he is square;
He may die early and dilate,
    And may be foul when fair.'

He may be fast when he is slow,
    And loose when he is tight,
And high when he is very low,
    And heavy when he's light.

He may be wet when he is dry,
    He may be great when small;
May purchase when he won't go by;
    Have naught when he has awl.

He may be sick when he is swell,
    And hot when he is cold;
He's skilled so he on earth may dwell,
    And when he's young he's old.

www.ingramcontent.com/pod-product-compliance
Lightning Source LLC
Chambersburg PA
CBHW020606030726
47497CB00007B/2112